The Vigilante: Six-Gun Law

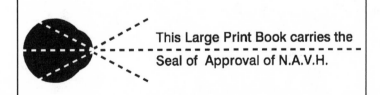

This Large Print Book carries the
Seal of Approval of N.A.V.H.

THE VIGILANTE: SIX-GUN LAW

JORY SHERMAN

THORNDIKE PRESS
A part of Gale, Cengage Learning

Detroit • New York • San Francisco • New Haven, Conn • Waterville, Maine • London

Copyright © 2006 by Jory Sherman.
Thorndike Press, a part of Gale, Cengage Learning.

ALL RIGHTS RESERVED
This is a work of fiction. Names, characters, places, and incidents either are the product of the author's imagination or are used fictitiously, and any resemblance to actual persons, living or dead, business establishments, events, or locales is entirely coincidental.
Thorndike Press® Large Print Western.
The text of this Large Print edition is unabridged.
Other aspects of the book may vary from the original edition.
Set in 16 pt. Plantin.
Printed on permanent paper.

LIBRARY OF CONGRESS CATALOGING-IN-PUBLICATION DATA

Sherman, Jory.
    The vigilante. Six-gun law / by Jory Sherman.
        p. cm. — (Thorndike Press large print Western)
    ISBN-13: 978-1-4104-0885-3 (hardcover : alk. paper)
    ISBN-10: 1-4104-0885-X (hardcover : alk. paper)
    1. Large type books. I. Title. II. Title: Six-gun law.
PS3569.H43V57 2008
813'.54—dc22   2008021271

Published in 2008 by arrangement with The Berkley Publishing Group, a member of Penguin Group (USA) Inc.

Printed in the United States of America
1 2 3 4 5 6 7 12 11 10 09 08

For Pat and Dusty Richards

1

He wore the gun all the time now. It had become a part of him and he carried it on his gunbelt as he had once carried a claw hammer when he was small, helping his father to nail boards together. The single-action Colt .45 lay under his pillow at night, was always close at hand. The loops in his gunbelt were filled with the gleaming bullets, like jewelry. He kept the pistol cleaned and oiled and he practiced with it almost every day. He had drawn it from its holster so many times that the leather inside was worn smooth, and he rubbed hog lard into the leather until the holster was as supple as a baby's soft skin.

There was a darkness in him after the killings, a stain that would not go away. No matter that he had saved the lives of two people, Edna and Twyman Butterfield, his friends and neighbors. No matter that the dead were two killers, Fritz Canby and

Wiley Pope, who had murdered his parents. Revenge had not been his motive. It was only justice that he sought, a justice that had been denied by a crooked sheriff in Alpena dancing to the tune of Wiley's father, Virgil Pope, and Fritz's father, Luke Canby, two of the most powerful men in Alpena, Arkansas. There was blood on his gun and he knew that his own life would be changed, shaped by forces beyond his control.

The threats he had gotten were all blunt. These were in the form of notes left at the store his parents had owned, tacked on his barn door during the night, nailed to his buggy.

Lew Wetzel Zane, you're a dead man for killing Wiley and Fritz.

Each note bore much the same message.

None of the notes were signed, but he had a pretty good idea who had written them. They were written in two different hands, with crude lettering. The handwriting was probably disguised. Canby and Pope. Or their wives. Nothing he could prove, and even if he could prove who wrote the notes, the law in Alpena, where both men lived, would do nothing. The sheriff there had not done anything about Fritz and Wiley, and an eyewitness had identified them as the murderers of Lew's parents. That eyewitness was later killed, too.

His neighbors, Edna and Twyman Butterfield, who now managed the store in Osage, had brought him the two most recent notes just yesterday, and these were even more ominous than the others. One had been left at the store; the other had been tacked on the Butterfields' front door.

Lew wasn't afraid, he was just careful. He no longer rode into Osage on the road, but traveled through the woods, where he was more comfortable. He had changed his habits and routines in the past two weeks. He went to the barn at different times. Before he went anywhere, he scanned the woods around the house, the field, the road. He looked and he listened. He waited. When he did move, he did not dawdle, but went quickly to the outhouse or the barn, the creek or the pond, and he never followed a straight line.

So far, so good, but he knew he had to make even more drastic changes in his life. And with a deep feeling of sadness, he knew he was going to have to leave Arkansas. He had to leave, he knew, or he would be forced to defend his life. He would be forced to kill again, just to survive.

The hardest part was going to be when he had to say good-bye to Seneca Jones. He had developed a fondness for her that threatened to lead to more passionate emotions. She was a beautiful young woman and they had grown close following the murder of his parents. The last time he had seen her, a week ago, there had been a brief flash in her eyes, when they were parting, that stirred something so deep inside him that he was startled, both by its suddenness and its intensity. It felt as if she had ignited a hidden cauldron in his loins that flowed like burning lava to his brain. Those blue eyes of hers had sparkled with a look that needed no words, a sultry look of longing, the smoking signal of a woman in season. She had told him, with that bold, quick look, that she wanted him, wanted him as a mate, wanted to take him to her bed at that very instant.

It had been unsettling, that look, and he had responded with an uncommon awkwardness, shuffling off her porch like a gangly kid still wet behind the ears. And not a word spoken. Not even "Good-bye." Just off into the night atop his horse for the long ride home from Possum Trot and feelings boiling inside him like a mysterious porridge, full of conflict and indecision.

Lew had made his painful decision to leave the Osage Valley before anyone else got hurt or killed. Now he waited for Edna and Twyman to show up at his place on their way into town to open the store. They had been minding it since the death of his parents, and he was grateful. But now it was just another millstone around his neck. He walked to the front room and looked out the side window toward the lane that streamed off the main road and led to his home. He had heard something, or thought he had, and he wanted to make sure.

He saw them, then, in their buggy, turning up his lane toward the little cemetery where his folks were buried. He walked to the dining room table and riffled through a sheaf of papers, then went to the back door to let the Butterfields in when they arrived. He did not have to wait long. He opened the door for them as their buggy came to a halt.

"Good morning, Lew," Edna said in a cheery tone of voice.

"Howdy, Lew." Twyman set the brake, swung down, then walked to the passenger side and helped Edna alight.

"Good morning," Lew said without any enthusiasm. He tried to smile, but such an action had to fight its way out of the darkness that was within him. Edna and Twyman didn't notice, however, as they were both reaching for the cigar box that was on the floor of the buggy. Twyman retrieved it, and the two walked to the door and entered the log home's kitchen.

"We brought the week's receipts, Lew," Edna said. "I guess you wanted us to bring them, along with the money we took in last week."

"Let's sit in the dining room," Lew said.

They all sat at the table. Twyman set the cigar box in front of him. Both he and Edna looked at the papers at the place where Lew sat.

"I won't be needing what you brought, Twy," Lew said. "I've got some legal papers here I want you both to look at. If they meet with your approval, we'll all sign them."

"What are they?" Edna asked, a note of suspicion in her voice.

"I'm turning the store over to you and Twyman, Edna. I'm leaving Osage."

"Leaving Osage? Why?"

"I think you know why. I don't want any more run-ins with the Popes or the Canbys."

"This is terrible," Twyman said. "This is your home. What about your place here?"

"I saw a banker in Berryville the other day. I told him I wanted to sell my place. He bought it right then and there, said he could

12

sell it easily. He paid me and said it was a good investment for him."

Both Edna and Twyman reeled back in their chairs, their mouths open in disbelief.

"Read the papers. And please keep this to yourselves until after I've gone."

"When are you planning to leave?" Edna asked.

"In a week or so. I should be ready by then."

He shoved duplicate sets of legal papers toward both Twyman and Edna. They started reading.

"I'm taking my horse, leaving the other stock to you, as well," Lew said.

"You're just giving us the store?" Twyman said. "You don't want no money for it?"

"I am. No strings attached. I think Ma and Pa would approve."

"But that store is worth good money," Edna said.

"Not to me," Lew said. "Do you want it?"

"Why, yes, but this is all so sudden. I can't believe you're just giving us the store your folks built up and . . ."

"Please," Lew said. "I'll feel better about going away if you own it. And my stock here. You can have the wagon and the buggy, too. It's all in those papers, giving you ownership."

"I know," Twyman said. "I just can't get over it. Are you real sure, Lew?"

"Dead sure," Lew said with a laconic twist to his lips. "Just sign the papers and I'll sign them, too, and have them duly filed."

Edna's eyes started to leak tears as she signed the papers. Twyman choked on something in his throat when he put down his scrawl of a signature. Lew signed them and stood up.

"Thanks," he said. "I wish you prosperity and good health."

"Lew, oh, Lew," Edna wailed, "I can't believe you'd leave Osage. You grew up here. You've got friends. . . ."

"I know. It's best this way, Edna. Now, you two go on. I'll take care of these."

Lew watched the two walk numbly from the room and heard the back door slam. Good-byes were tough, and this was only the first of even tougher ones to come before he left the town. He felt a great weight lift from his shoulders. He had considered selling the store, but the Butterfields had been loyal friends to him and his folks and he knew they couldn't afford even to put up any earnest money for the store in Osage. He certainly didn't want to profit off them, considering all they had done over the years and after the murder of his parents.

He heard the buggy creak as it turned and rolled down the road. He drew in a deep breath and clenched his teeth. There was still so much to do.

And the hardest part would be telling Seneca that he was leaving.

2

Late in the afternoon, Lew saddled Ruben and rode into Osage. As he crossed the bridge over the creek, Ruben's hooves rang hollow on the wood. He would miss that sound, he knew. There were so many things he had taken for granted in that long valley. But now he paid close attention to everything, knowing that all that he loved here would vanish, be consigned to memory, and then even the memory would fade into wisps of fog that would blow away like cobwebs in a high wind.

He intended to ride straight through town to Possum Trot, on his way to see Seneca, but he caught sight of Don Swanson, the sheriff, who hailed him and waved him over to his small office across the street from the general store. Lew turned his horse and waved back, relieved that he could delay saying farewell to Seneca for a while longer.

"Don," Lew said as he rode up.

"Ridin' up to see Ed Jones?" Swanson said. His black trotter, Nox, was tied to the hitch rail in front of his office. Swanson looked at the pistol on Lew's hip, squinted his eyes. He wore no side arm, seldom did.

"Well, to see Seneca, yes."

"Got a minute?"

"Sure."

"Come on in. Something I want to talk to you about before you go up there."

Lew wrapped his reins around the rail, patting Ruben on the rump as he followed Swanson up the steps and into his office.

"Have a chair, Lew."

Swanson walked around his desk and sat down. The desk was clean. There was little crime in Osage, and what there was didn't involve a lot of paperwork.

"I see you're packing a new Colt, Lew."

"Shorter barrel, bigger punch. Lighter than the old .44/40, Don."

"You huntin' snakes?"

"There's a passel of 'em this time of year."

"Makes me no nevermind. I don't much like snakes myself."

"You call me in here to talk about killing snakes, Don?"

"Something I want to show you. First, though, I got a question."

"Go ahead."

17

"You still friends with Danny Slater, Bobby Gleason, and Kevin Smith? I know you went to school with those boys and they were real close to your brother, David."

"I haven't seen much of them since my folks' funeral, tell the truth. Why?"

"I got 'em in the back. Want you to talk to them, see what they have to say."

"They're in jail?"

"Well, this ain't really no jail, Lew. Y'know. More like a storeroom I got back there."

"It's a jail."

"All right."

"What'd they do?"

Swanson pulled open a drawer in his desk. The wood made a screeching sound. He reached in and pulled out three bills. He laid these on the desk, spread them out evenly, one next to the other. He looked at the bills for a moment, then at Lew.

"Yesterday, the church had a horseshoe-pitching contest and a feed. Lots of people came down out of the hills. Way for the church to raise some money. I spotted Virgil Pope and Luke Canby there. Pretty good horseshoe players."

Lew stiffened at the mention of those two names.

"Well, real late in the day, when the church folks were cleanin' up, there was old

Virg and Luke over talkin' to them three boys. Real serious like. And them boys was noddin' their heads and listenin' real serious. Then I seen Virg and Luke dig into their pockets and hand something to the boys. They all shook hands. Luke and Virg rode on back to Alpena. I got up real early this mornin', come down here with Nox and kept out of sight, but right near that window yonder. Had me a real strong hunch, Lew. Real strong."

"Good story, Don, but what's the damned point?"

"Now, now, don't you get your dander up, Lew. I'm gettin' to it."

Lew slumped back in his chair, waited for the rest of the story.

"This mornin', I seen the three young'uns ride through. I caught up to 'em on the bridge and asked 'em where they was goin'. They said they was goin' fishin', but I told them I didn't see no poles ner bait, nary a can of crawlers, nothin' like that. But each of them boys had a rifle with them and I asked if they was goin' to shoot fish. They said they might hunt some squirrels and could cut some cane poles over to the Blue Hole. More I talked to them, more their stories drifted away from fishin' at the Blue Hole. I made them turn out their pockets.

19

Each of 'em had one of these bills. Take a look at them, Lew. Look real close."

Lew stood up, leaned over the desk. His eyes widened.

"Those are hundred-dollar bills, Don."

Swanson smiled.

Lew sat back down.

"I told them boys I knew where they got the money and they all turned right sheepish. You wanta know what they told me?"

"I can't even guess," Lew said.

"Said Virgil and Luke gave them bills to them to put your lamp out, Lew. Said they was to get another hunnert each after they done the deed."

"They were going to kill me?" Lew said.

Swanson smiled again.

"Naw, they said they just took the money because it was free. They told me they was a-goin' to ride on over to your place and tell you to git."

"You didn't believe them, I take it," Lew said.

"Thought I'd let you decide that, Lew. They're friends of your'n. Let's go on back and see what those boys have to say."

"All right," Lew said. The skin on the back of his neck prickled.

"You can't wear that hogleg back there,

though. Better give it to me for safekeeping."

Lew looked into the sheriff's eyes, as if searching for any smoke of deception. Swanson's eyes were steady on his. Lew pulled the Colt from its holster and handed it across the desk.

"You trust me?" Swanson said.

"Up to a point," Lew admitted.

A brief smile flickered across the sheriff's face.

"The way it's lookin', you might not have too many folks you can trust, Lew."

Lew said nothing. He followed the sheriff as Swanson unlocked the door to the back part of the small building. They walked down a hallway, through another room. Swanson unlocked still another door made of heavy oak.

"Comin' in, boys," Swanson said as he pulled the door open.

The room had built-in bunks, a table, no chairs, a single bench along one wall. The three young men were sitting on it, looking like a trio of owls, their eyes wide and bright, teary from the sudden light. There was one high window with bars on it. Feeble sunlight trickled through it, tiny motes dancing in the small shafts.

"Hey, Lew," Danny said. "Looks like we

stepped into some shit."

"I just want to know one thing," Lew said. "Were you going to shoot me?"

"Naw, Lew. We was just goin' to tell you what old Virgil and Luke Canby wanted us to do so's you could light a shuck."

"Then, what were you going to tell Pope and Canby?"

"We was going to tell them you run off," Bobby said. "Honest."

"That right, Kevin?" Lew said.

"That's plumb right, Lew. You know we wouldn't do nothin' to you no ways. We just took the money they gave us."

"I don't believe you. Sheriff says you had rifles with you."

"We had to make it look good," Bobby said. "Case somebody said something to Pope and Canby. They're plumb riled that you killed their boys."

"Those boys would be alive today if that damned Alpena sheriff had arrested them. Billy Jim Colfax has got the balls of a field mouse."

"They'd be in prison," Slater said.

"Was Sheriff Colfax in on this?" Lew asked.

The three boys shrugged.

"Now, Lew," Swanson said, "you don't want to widen your loop too much."

"I think Colfax knows what Canby and Pope are up to," Lew said. "Three peas in a pod."

"Well," Gleason said, "Virgil did say we'd have no trouble with the law if we done you in."

"You can make it plainer than that, Bobby."

Gleason stood up. The sunlight splashed the top of his head, gilding the hairs with a pale buttery light.

"All right. Virgil said Billy Jim would look the other way."

"What about me?" Swanson asked. "Did he say that I would turn my back on a killing?"

"No, sir," Gleason said.

"He said to let him know if you gave us any trouble and he'd take care of it," Smith said.

"And what did you think he meant by that, Kevin?" Swanson said.

Smith shrugged. "I didn't think about it. I told you, Sheriff, we wasn't going to kill Lew."

"Did you think I'd run, Kevin?" Lew asked. There was iron in his voice and he fixed Smith with a piercing stare.

None of the young men answered. Kevin looked down at his feet and started raking one shoe across the pine flooring as if there was a stain there that wouldn't come out. Gleason sucked in a breath, and Slater looked away to a corner of the room.

Lew turned to Swanson.

"I've heard enough, Don. Let's go."

Swanson gave the boys a scathing glance.

"Sorry, boys," he said.

"You going to press charges, Lew?" Slater asked, a pleading whine in his voice.

Lew didn't answer. He walked out of the room. The sheriff locked the door. The young men ran to it and started pounding on it.

"Come on, Lew. We're your friends," Bobby yelled. "We want to go home."

The trio was still yelling when Swanson and Lew entered the office. Swanson locked the door, went behind his desk.

"I'll have my pistol back now, Don," Lew said.

Swanson hesitated. "I don't know if I should give it to you. You're mad enough to use it on someone. I can tell."

"I'm going to see Seneca, that's all."

"Don't do anything foolish, Lew. You can't take the law into your own hands."

He handed the Colt back to Lew. Lew slid it back in its holster.

"What law is that, Don?"

"Let's not go through all that again. I do the best I can here."

"What about Colfax?"

"He's duly sworn."

"Shit."

"Now, don't go off half-cocked on Billy Jim. He ain't in this, far as I can see. I could make out a charge against Pope and Canby, but I doubt if the judge would do anything. It would be those boys' word against theirs and they'd deny they paid to have you murdered. And if the judge finds that no law has been broken, exactly, Colfax can't arrest Virgil or Luke, and neither can I."

"Nobody wants to buck Pope and Canby, Don. That's what you're saying."

"Well, I don't think even a jury would believe those boys. What do you think I ought to do with them?"

"What did you have in mind, Don?"

"Maybe disorderly conduct. Ten days in the Alpena jail."

Lew snorted.

"About all I can do, without stirring up a lot of trouble up there."

"In Alpena, you mean."

"Yes."

"Suit yourself. I think my friends need time to think about what they've done. Or what they might have done."

"Yeah. I agree."

Lew stood up.

"You know what bothers me about all this, Don?"

"I reckon you feel betrayed by your friends."

Lew started for the door.

"I'm thinking that I might have had to kill three of my best friends, Don. That's what's itching right under my skin."

Sheriff Don Swanson shivered in his chair as if gripped by a sudden chill.

He had no doubt that Lew meant every word he said.

3

As Lew climbed into the saddle, Sheriff Swanson stepped out on the porch. He held up the three one-hundred-dollar bills, flapped them up and down.

"Zane," Swanson said. "You watch your back, hear?"

Lew nodded, touched a finger to the brim of his hat, and turned Ruben toward the Possum Trot road.

Shadows stretched eastward in long stripes from the trees. His own shadow rippled on the road like oil floating on water. Grasshoppers made brittle sounds with their wings as they broke cover and took flight ahead of him.

Lew felt sorry for the three boys in jail. They had been his brother David's best friends before David had drowned, and he felt a special kinship with them, as if they were living links to David. Whether or not they had meant to kill him for money, he did not know. He knew that a hundred-dollar bill was a lot of money to folks born poor. That's what galled him more than anything, that Virgil and Luke had tempted the boys. They had waved money at them, knowing that the money could corrupt almost anyone, especially young fellows who didn't have better sense.

He turned his horse onto the rough-hewn road that led to the Jones house, the scent of cedar strong in his nostrils, the june bugs hopping off the road into the grasshopper country of tall weeds and old blackberry vines. His shadow crept up the slope toward the house as the sun hung just over the western horizon, frozen there for one last blaze of fiery glory.

The road was a maze of horse tracks, none of which looked familiar to him. Despite his preoccupation with seeing Seneca again, bidding her farewell, his mind was drawn to the hoof marks. He began to decipher them from long habit, as a man who composes music might begin to hum notes scrawled on a page of scales, or a retired mathematician might follow a formula found in an old textbook. Reading signs came natural to Lew, for he had lived outdoors, in the woods, for most of his young life and followed in the footsteps of his guiding father, who had taught him all he knew about tracking animal or man.

Two sets of horse tracks ascending the road, three coming back down. And fresh, all of the hoof marks were fresh, less than an hour old, he surmised. Visitors? Ed Jones, as most of the people who lived on Possum Trot, had few visitors, and then only when he was making sorghum. And in this time of summer, Ed was not manufacturing syrup, but tending to his cane.

The sun dropped below the horizon and Lew turned back to look at its last flare, the loaves of clouds floating like salmon just above the treetops, then turning ashen and cold as the light failed and the sky began to darken. Something his father had told him more than once came to mind: "Never miss a sunrise or a sunset, son." It was an axiom that Lew had followed once he understood what his father had meant.

"Each morning that you go out of the house just before dawn," Del Zane had said, "you are witness to creation itself. The birth of a new day. Each day like no other. And to see a blazing sunset is to see the Father of us all painting his masterpieces, evening after evening unto eternity."

His father's words stayed with him and became part of the fabric of his life. They seemed even more important, more sacred, even, since his father's death. Yes, he thought, sacred was the word. His father, Delbert Zane, had been his guide for nineteen years, teaching him, warning him, leading him on a deep spiritual path without being ecclesiastic or domineering. With soft words, words that Lew continued to hear as if they were just spoken into his ear, just breathed into his consciousness a moment ago.

The house was dark, and Lew was surprised. Stars were beginning to stipple the sky like flung diamonds and the trees had gathered up their shadows and created dark sculptures around their trunks.

Seneca should have lighted a lamp by then, Lew thought. The windows in the front room should have been shimmering with a pale golden light, and most certainly, there should have been a lamp lighted in the kitchen, and maybe one in the dining room.

Ruben's ears pricked to hard cones and twisted back and forth as Lew topped the rise to the house, the hitch rail barely visible, a shiny post that held the light enough for him to see it.

"What's the matter, boy?" Lew said, his voice soft and without tremor. "Something wrong?"

Lew swung out of the saddle. The creak of leather was loud in the deep silence of the evening. He wrapped the reins around the hitch rail and stood there, looking at the porch, the dark house, the froed shingled roof. Everything so quiet, he thought. Everything so *unnaturally* quiet. Not even a cricket scraping its legs, nor the leathery lash of the whippoorwill's tongue announcing that the night was upon them and owls were floating like wraiths through the cedars, the oaks, and the hickory trees.

So quiet his nerves crackled like bacon skittering in a skillet of hot grease.

"Ed," Lew called, his right hand dropping to the butt of his Colt.

There was no answer.

"Seneca?"

The thick trees bordering the back lot of the house seemed to swallow his words. The silence became even more deafening as his voice died away into nothingness.

Lew looked around as if to determine if any of the nearby shadows were moving. Stillness and motionless. He felt as if he were in a cave, isolated from all life. A dark cave, where only he and Ruben stood, as if on an island of pure silence, a small piece of land devoid of all beings.

31

Be careful, a small voice inside him warned.

Those tracks might mean something. Something ominous. Something that could fill a cautious man with dread.

Lew walked to the front steps, stopping after each footfall, to listen. He put a foot on the first step, waited. Then he inched forward, putting his weight on that foot, pulled the other one forward, for balance. He went to the next step, and the next, until he stood on the porch. The oak planks had hardened over the years and the boards on the porch did not creak.

"Seneca?" Lew called again.

He turned toward the front door and took a step.

The hackles on the back of his neck prickled when he saw that the door was slightly ajar.

"Ed, you home? Seneca? Anybody?"

Lew drew his pistol. It whispered out of the holster. The sound sent a shiver up his spine. He stepped forward and pushed the door all the way open. The metal hinges squeaked ever so soft, like the far-off peep of a baby chick. Inside, he saw only darkness, heard only more silence, a deeper silence now. The lonesome silence of an empty house.

"Ed? Anybody home in there?"

Lew stiffened. He thought he heard a sound. What was it? A groan? A moan? His imagination?

"Ed? It's me, Lew Zane."

He heard a scuffling. More groans. He had not imagined them. The hairs on the back of his neck subsided, replaced by a hard cold ball of iron in his stomach.

Lew hunched over and stepped through the door, his finger on the pistol hammer, ready to cock the single-action with a downward press.

He sidled left, away from the door, and struck a small table that he had forgotten was there. He stifled a curse and flattened himself against the wall.

"Ed? You in there?"

"Mmmf. Mmmmmf."

Down the hall. The kitchen, maybe. His senses prickled as if he had walked across a rug in winter and touched something metal; as if electrified by a sudden spark set off by friction.

"Ed?"

Sounds of scuffling and then a heavy pounding. Lew stiffened and eased the hammer back on the Colt. The metallic click as the mechanism engaged the sear sounded throughout the house, so loud he was sure the world had heard it.

The heavy blows ceased and the house filled with silence once again.

He walked toward the hallway, only dimly visible in the shadowy confines of the front room. He stepped softly down the hall, past a closed door. He entered the small dining room, and then he was in the kitchen.

"Mmmmmf."

Lew whirled at the sound and went into a fighting crouch, the pistol held level in front of him. He was a tiger, ready to pounce.

Nobody rushed him.

"Ed? You in here?"

"Uhhhnhhnhhh." A long sound, this time, from a corner of the room. Over by the iron cookstove, he thought.

Then, the thud of something heavy on the hardwood flooring. Lew's finger trembled near the trigger.

"Uhhhumffff."

Lew eased the hammer back down to half-cock and strode toward the source of the sounds. He stepped into a blob of darkness, then felt the cold iron of the stove on his hip. He stretched a foot out and his boot struck something soft, softer than the floor, but harder than just a bundle of clothes.

"Ed?" He said the name with a tone just above a whisper.

"Uhmf."

Lew bent down and reached out with his left hand. He felt something. Something alive. He patted the object and knew what it was. A foot. A shoe. He moved his hands both ways, and felt a leg, felt something around one ankle, something corded and familiar. Rope.

"Is this you, Ed?"

"Uhhhmmmffff." Savagely positive, this time, the voice loud, insistent. Desperate.

"Hold on. I'll light a lamp."

"Nnnnnmmmffff."

"All right. Wait."

Lew holstered his pistol and felt along the trousers, to the waist. Then, with both hands, he probed the figure on the floor until he felt bare skin. A chin, a cheek, cloth tight around the mouth. He followed the path of the cloth and his fingers detected a knot. He used both hands to untie the knot and pulled the cloth free.

"Lew, goddamnit, untie me, quick."

"I can't see a damned thing, Ed."

"My hands. Untie my hands."

He felt Ed's body lurch as he lunged to one side. Lew let his hands find the rope around Ed's wrists and he began to untie them. The rope came free and Ed sat up. He was close enough now to see him, not his face, but his human shape. Ed's fingers worked frantically at the ropes around his legs and ankles.

"Sonofabitch," Ed said as Lew heard the plunk of the rope falling to the floor. "Help me up, Lew. I'll get us some light."

Lew stood up and slid his hands beneath Ed's arms, helped him to his feet. He stood there as Ed hobbled off somewhere. Scratching sounds, a soft clank of metal, a tink of glass. Then another scratch and Lew saw a blossom of orange flame, the dim flash of Ed's face as he lit the lamp. He turned up the wick and Ed's features and his body sprang into view, the kitchen burst out in sudden relief and the darkness fled.

"What the hell happened here, Ed?"

Lew stepped toward him. Ed's hands were shaking, his fingers trembling as if he was gripped with palsy.

"She — she's gone," Ed said. "They got Seneca, the bastards."

Lew stood there, staring at Ed's eyes, eyes that were wet with tears. He felt as if someone had just struck him full in the chest with a sixteen-pound maul. All of the air was gone out of his lungs and he couldn't drag any back in.

And that cold iron ball in his stomach swelled to a gigantic mass, freezing his senses as if he had been plunged into an icy river.

Lew felt as if he were drowning in those gelid waters off some snowy Alaskan coast and he was in a torrent racing him out to some bottomless Arctic sea where all was blackness and bereft of all hope.

4

Ed Jones stood there on wobbly legs, his lower lip swollen and caked with dried blood. He touched a lump on his forehead, just below the hairline on the right side of his face. He winced and took his hand away.

Lew looked at him with narrowed eyes, then shifted his gaze to the back door, the streams of tracked-in dirt on the floor. The door was open, gaping as if some untold story lay just beyond, out there in the darkness.

"What happened, Ed? Where's Seneca? You said they took her. Who? When?"

Ed leaned back against the counter to steady himself. He rubbed one wrist, then the other. The ropes had left deep indentations in his skin, bloodless lattice patterns attesting to the tightness of his bonds.

"They jumped me, musta been a coupla hours ago. Virgil Pope and Luke Canby. Out back, as I was comin' back in from the privy.

Whacked me good, tied me like a damned Christmas turkey, and waited for Seneca to come back in from milkin'. Put a gag in my mouth so's I couldn't warn her they was here."

"They took Seneca?"

"Said if she didn't go with 'em, they'd shoot me dead. I gotta ride down now and tell Swanson what they done."

Lew felt the anger rise in him like a boil swelling to a redness just before it bursts.

"Ed, they must have given you a reason why they took Seneca. She's done them no harm."

"Oh, yeah, Lew. They took her because they want you. Told me to give you a message. And I hate like hell to give it to you, but my daughter means the world to me and they got her. Took her up to Alpena, said you could come get her."

"You're damned right I'll go and get her, Ed."

"I ought to go with you. But I gotta tell Sheriff Swanson so's he'll go after 'em and arrest them for kidnapping my daughter. I think they mean to kill you for shooting down their boys. They're plumb mad at you, Lew, for what you done."

"Those boys murdered my folks, Ed, and they got what they deserved. They tried to kill me, remember?"

"I know, I know. Lew, this is turning into such a mess I don't know where to start in. They got my girl and I itch all over to get her back before they do something to her just to get at you."

Lew raised his hands, pressed them together, held them to his lips. He bowed his head, not to pray, but to think. He hadn't foreseen this. He knew that Pope and Canby hated him for killing their sons, but he had acted in self-defense. If the law had gone after those two murderers, as it should have, Wiley and Fritz would still be alive. They would be in prison, but they would be alive.

He had no doubt that Pope and Canby were behind all the threats he had been getting, and they had even tried to hire his friends to kill him. They were desperate men, so desperate that they had kidnapped an innocent girl and were using her as bait so that they could kill him. Revenge. That's what those two men wanted. And Seneca was the pawn in their deadly game.

"I'll get her back, Ed."

"I — I'm going with you, Lew."

"No, you better not. I'll go it alone."

"Why not? I owe it to my daughter to rescue her from those brigands."

"Brigands? They're worse than that, Ed.

40

And you'd best not come with me because they're not going to give Seneca up without a fight."

"That's why I want to go."

"And that's just why you can't. You're liable to either get killed or arrested. Those two are gunning for me. I'll make it easy on them."

"There's two of them and only one of you. Lew, I've got to go with you. If for no other reason than to even up the odds."

"Look, Ed, Pope and Canby mean business. I wouldn't put it past them to have the Alpena sheriff in on this."

"That's three against one."

Lew pressed his lips together like a fist.

"Maybe more," Lew said.

Ed pushed away from the counter, tried to stand straight. But his legs wouldn't let him. One of them wobbled and started to give way. Lew walked over to him, put his hands on his shoulders.

"You're in no shape to ride all the way up to Alpena, Ed."

"No — no, I can make it. I'll get my rifle and pistol, saddle old Mose and —"

Lew cut him off.

"Best thing you can do is put some liniment on places where it hurts, Ed. If you want to be useful, you can maybe ride down to Osage and tell Sheriff Swanson what happened. It probably won't do any good, but it's better than nothing."

"Yeah, I could do that."

Lew took his hands away. Ed wobbled some, but didn't fall down.

"Why do you say it won't do any good to tell Sheriff Swanson what happened?"

"Because the law doesn't mean anything around here. Maybe all over. The people put a badge on a man and expect him to protect them. The man gets the badge, struts around like a damned peacock, and runs when trouble comes along. Making a man a sheriff just gives him more power than he deserves and doesn't do anything for the law."

"Just because Sheriff Colfax did you a bad turn, Lew, doesn't mean they're all corrupt. Don's been a pretty decent man, to my way of thinking."

"Don doesn't have any power in a little old town like Osage. He's supposed to keep the peace, and I reckon he does that. But if he rides outside the city limits, he's just another farmer from Osage."

"You may be right. I'll ride down there and tell him about Seneca. Maybe he'll know what to do."

"Oh, he knows what to do, but if he goes

up to Alpena, Colfax will back him down just like he did before when those boys killed my folks. Look, Ed, I'm going. We've already wasted too much time. You get well before you do any riding, hear?"

"I'm all right, Lew."

"If you say so. But stay the hell away from Alpena. I mean it."

"I will," Ed promised.

Lew stalked through the kitchen and out the front door. Moonlight glazed the land, the leaves of the trees. He set off down the Possum Trot trail, heading for Osage.

There probably was a shorter way to Alpena, but he didn't know those parts of the hills beyond Possum Trot. Only a few did. There were so many roads, only a born native knew where they led. In the dark, anyway, and it was pitch dark. Clouds had moved in to obscure the moon and stars, and in the air, when he sniffed, there was the distinct tang of an oncoming storm. The air was full of moisture as if the earth was gathering a head of steam for one hell of a rainstorm.

Lew did not cross the creek after he left Osage, but rode along the creek. There would be some fences to jump, he knew, but Pope and Canby could be waiting for

43

him on the Alpena road. In the distance, he heard the faint rumble of thunder, and wished that he had thought to tie on a slicker behind his saddle. He kept the road in sight when he could, but he saw no sign of anyone. The road was quiet, deserted.

When he got to Carrolton, he crossed the creek and took Ruben back on the road. The sky to the north flashed with far-off lightning, followed by rumbling peals of thunder. As he rode north, he counted the seconds between the flashes and the sound of thunder, figuring the distance before the storm hit. One second was roughly equal to a mile. One slow second.

The air had thickened so that he could almost swallow it, it was so wet. The lightning flashes got closer, but he had only a few short miles to go before he came to the crossroads. Where, he wondered, would Pope and Canby have taken Seneca? To the lumberyard? Or to Canby's hardware store? He would check the hardware store first. It was the handiest.

Ruben started dancing as they came into the blacked-out town. Heavy black clouds swarmed overhead like elephants. Jagged veins of lightning streaked through some of them still off to the north, etching a broken lattice of mercury for just a brief moment.

The thunder boomed so close, he couldn't finish his count. Less than a mile away, and there was death in those lightning strikes that pierced the ground like ragged silver lances. Ruben was as skittery as a newborn colt, prancing right and left, wanting to fight the bit and run to shelter.

Lew came to the crossroads, saw the dark lumberyard off to the left. The rail tracks glistened like molten silver with each flash of lightning. And he heard the rain, stalking across the land with a steady tattoo that became a single sound, water rushing down a spout. He turned to the right, toward the hardware store in the next block. The rain caught up to him, and a gust of wind lashed him, splashing his face with freshets of water, brisk, but not yet cold. The rain stung his eyes and he wiped them with two fingers drawn across the lids. The darkness seemed to close in on him, enveloping him in a wet shroud.

He saw a light in the back of the store as he approached. A lamp was burning and that meant that someone was inside. There were no horses at the hitch rail out front, but he had not expected Pope and Canby would make it easy for him. Yet he was sure that they wanted him to come after Seneca. Why hide the horses?

He circled the block and came in at the rear of the store. Light spilled from a back window, a pale yellow glow that illuminated the back steps to the loading dock. And there, he saw three horses tied to posts, their saddles slick and shiny with fresh rain. The horses switched their tails as if trying to bat the raindrops away like so many flies, and Lew's heart leaped in his chest.

Seneca was surely inside, he thought, and his next move was to figure out how to get in and not get killed before he even fired a shot.

He kept on going, past the store, and found a place to tie up Ruben. He slipped his rifle from its sheath and stalked back up the alleyway, walking slow, looking at every clump of shadow, listening for sounds through the insistent sawing of the rain on his hat, the ground, the roofs, the wooden sides of buildings.

He reached the loading dock and stepped carefully up the stairs until he was level with the window. He drew close and peered inside. There was a wall blocking his view of the back room of the store. He put his ear to the pane and listened.

He heard voices, tried to decipher the words.

"— anytime now, Virg."

"Check the front again, Luke." Pope's voice this time.

"Aw, he won't come in that way."

"Then, check the back, damn it."

Lew stepped away from the window, froze his body to the back wall, next to the door. He could barely hear the sound of boots on the hardwood flooring. The light in the window shuddered and broke up as a body passed close to the pane. The dock plunged into darkness for a few seconds; then the light wavered again as Canby walked past the window to the door. Lew heard the latch rattle, as if Luke was testing to see if it was still locked.

Then, silence.

Canby was still at the door. Lew heard the sound of pressure on the wood.

He figured Canby was pressing his ear to the door, listening for any alien sounds.

Lew held his breath, his right hand gripping the butt of his pistol.

His heart jumped when he heard Seneca scream. The sound pierced his eardrums and all traces of the rain faded into the background.

Then Lew moved, his muscles bunching, his eyes narrowed to burning slits.

And Seneca screamed again.

5

Lew leaned his rifle against the back wall. He charged the door, grasping the latch. He gave a mighty tug, then slammed his shoulder into the door. He felt it give way as the echoes of Seneca's screams died away. He heard an angry grunt from Canby, then an explosion that blasted his eardrums, deafened him.

The door fell inward, sagging from the lower hinge. Canby grappled with him, tried to club Lew with the butt of the pistol he held in his hand.

A shout from the other room. Lew recognized the voice as Pope's.

"Shut up," Pope yelled at Seneca.

Luke Canby was strong, stronger than Lew. Lew grabbed the wrist with the gun, trying to force Canby to drop his weapon. Canby grunted and blew hot breath in Lew's face. His muscles corded up, giving him enough strength to resist. Lew was panting from the wrestling effort, but he held on. He danced Canby to one side, then brought a knee up into his groin.

Canby groaned and doubled over, but he sprang back swinging. The fist with the pistol in it struck Lew on the cheekbone, driving a sharp pain into his face, almost paralyzing it for a second. Stars danced like silver lightning bugs in Lew's brain and he staggered under the impact of the powerful blow. He regained his footing in time to throw up an arm and ward off still another blow, as Canby drove his pistol down toward Lew's head. Lew felt the air rush past his ear as Canby's arm completed its arc, brushing only against the brim of Lew's hat.

"Luke, what the hell's goin' on out there?" Pope yelled.

"Damned Zane," Canby spat, almost out of breath.

"You stay put, gal," Pope shouted.

Lew heard footsteps pounding on the hardwood flooring.

He doubled up a fist and threw an uppercut at Canby. He struck the man just under the chin. Canby's head snapped back, and his eyes rolled like errant marbles in their sockets.

Lew followed up his advantage, grabbed Canby's wrist, and wrested the pistol loose from his grip. Canby fought back, clawing at Lew's eyes, grabbing at the pistol. The two men tugged back and forth. Then Lew heard a click as Canby thumbed the hammer back. He heard the cylinder turn and snap into place on a fresh round. He pushed on Canby's arm, trying to keep the pistol from being turned on him. The pistol turned, pointed toward Canby at chest level.

There was an explosion just as Pope rounded the corner and entered the back room. Lew felt the pistol jump into his hand, as Canby's grip loosened. Canby staggered backward, a hole in his chest, a hole that gushed blood with every beat of his heart. Canby's eyes widened with shock. He lifted a hand to his chest and blood spurted through his fingers.

Lew grabbed the pistol, thumbed back the hammer. He whirled to face Pope, who was leveling a pistol at him.

Both men fired at the same time. Lew squeezed the trigger and ducked. He heard the sizzling whir of the bullet as it passed just over his head at nine hundred feet per second. Pope's slug caught Canby in the center of his throat and he went down like a sack of grain, gurgling out his last breath.

Lew's bullet made a smacking sound as it struck Pope's abdomen. Pope doubled over, gasping for air, as the wind was knocked out of his lungs.

"You . . . you bastard," Pope rasped, clutching the wound. Blood threaded his fingers and he sat down, his face blanched with pain, his mouth moving with silent curses.

Lew cocked Canby's pistol again and stepped over to Pope, looked down at him.

"You brought this on yourself, Pope."

"Damn you, Zane. Damn you for killing my son."

"Looks to me like he was cut from the same bolt as you, Pope. He tried to kill me. Just like you."

Pope struggled to lift his pistol for another shot at Lew.

Lew raised his leg and brought it straight down on Pope's wrist, forcing it to the floor. He stood on it with his full weight. He heard the sound of small bones crunching. The pistol slipped from Pope's grip and clattered on the floor. Pope gasped in pain. He didn't have enough wind to scream. Sweat bathed his face and tears streamed from his eyes.

"Ahh," Pope said. He doubled over and groaned.

Lew kicked Pope's pistol well away from him, clear past the partition that shielded the back room where Seneca was held captive.

"Lew?" Seneca called to him from the next room. "Lew, are you alive?"

"I'm here, Seneca. Be a minute."

"Are they — are they both dead?"

"Pert near," he said.

He dashed around the partition and into the next room, a storeroom and office. There were shelves stacked with boxes, nail kegs beneath, a desk, two chairs. Seneca was tied to a chair, her feet bound together, rope around her waist and arms. Lew shoved Canby's pistol into his belt and began untying the knots.

"They didn't even use new rope on you," he said, still panting slightly from the exertion of a few moments before. "This is an old horse rope."

"Oh, Lew, thank God you came. How did you know? Is my daddy all right?"

"He's fine."

"They wanted you to come after me. That's all they talked about. All the way up here and after they tied me up. Virgil, he started getting familiar with me. I screamed."

"I know. I heard you."

"They're bad men."

Lew finished untying the last knot, which

52

was behind her and held the rope at her ankles as well as the one around her waist and arms. He loosened the rope and Seneca sat there, rubbing her arms. She bent down and massaged both ankles.

"I'll take you back home," he said. "Soon as you're ready."

She started to say something, and then both of them froze as they heard a scraping sound. Lew whirled and saw Virgil Pope crawling toward him. He had picked up the pistol Lew had kicked away. He raised it and thumbed back the hammer.

"I — I thought they were both dead," Seneca said, her voice flat and toneless, as if she were half asleep. That was the fear, Lew knew.

Pope leveled the pistol. His entire midsection was wet with blood and Lew could smell his intestines, which were starting to bulge out of his abdomen. A bullet had torn through it, releasing the gases and the stench.

"I ain't dead yet, Zane," Pope rasped. His finger tightened on the trigger.

Lew's hand flashed toward his holster like a diving hawk. In a blur of speed, he jerked the Colt free, thumbing the hammer back as he brought it to bear on Pope.

Pope struggled to pull the trigger. Sweat

beaded up in the furrows on his forehead. His hand shook from pain and weakness. He gritted his teeth with the effort, as blood continued to stream from his gut. Finally, the trigger depressed and the pistol boomed, spewing out flame and sparks and hot lead.

At the same time, Lew fired his pistol, taking direct aim on an imaginary spot in the middle of Pope's forehead. The Colt bucked in his hand and he threw himself sideways. Pope's bullet shot past him and went into the main showroom of the hardware store. There was a *thunk* and then the sound of breaking glass as the bullet caromed off a plow blade and smashed through the front window.

Pope's forehead sprouted a blue-black hole and the back of his head exploded like a pie plate smashed with a rock. Brain matter flew like pasty cotton in all directions and the hole in his forehead sprouted a crimson flower. His eyes frosted over with the glaze of death and his neck sagged as all feeling went out of him. His head hit the floor with a resounding thud, and the blood from his forehead stopped flowing.

A pall of gray smoke hung in the air, swirled around the lighted lamp on the cluttered desk. Lew stood there, shaking inwardly, his thoughts scrambled, confused.

Killing Canby might have been an accident, but he had shot Pope right in the middle of his forehead without giving it a second thought. What had happened to him? Was it just animal instinct? A struggle for survival? He had killed again and there was no question in his mind that he had meant to put Pope's lamp out. Permanently.

"Lew — are you — are you all right?" Seneca asked, still frozen, standing stiffly in front of the chair that had been her prison.

"I — I don't know."

"What's wrong?"

"I guess I got buck fever."

"Buck fever?"

"I just killed a man, Seneca. It feels like the floor just dropped out from under me. It's an awful feeling."

She walked over to him, grabbed his arm with both hands. She squeezed him in an attempt to offer reassurance.

"He tried to kill you, Lew. You were just defending yourself."

Her words didn't help. He knew she wouldn't understand. That shot he had made had been deadly accurate. He had taken another human life and it was making his insides crawl, as if he had swallowed a gallon jug of spiders.

"Let's get out of here, Seneca." He holstered his pistol. "I'll take you back home."

She shivered against him and released her grip on his arm.

"I can't wait to see Daddy. I can't believe all this happened. Are you sure Virgil's dead? What about Mr. Canby?"

"He's dead, too. Come on. Let's go out the back and get your horse. Mine's out there, too."

Just then, they heard a crash out front as if someone was kicking the door in. There was a tinkle of glass and then they heard footsteps. Cautious footsteps, as if someone had just stepped inside.

Lew pushed Seneca around behind him.

"Wait here," he whispered.

He walked over to the wall and peered around it.

There, in the front of the store, stood the sheriff. Billy Jim Colfax. And he had a sawed-off double-barreled Greener in his hand. The shattered glass door hung open, gaping into the night.

Lew eased his pistol out of his holster. It barely made a sound.

Colfax went into a crouch.

"Luke? You back there?" Colfax's voice made a hollow echo in the empty store.

Lew didn't answer.

"Virgil? You get Zane?"

56

Lew waited, holding his breath.

"Zane, if that's you back there, I'm going to take you down."

"You go to hell, Billy Jim," Lew said. "Virgil and Luke are dead. If you're their hired gun, you're breaking the law if you come after me. It was self-defense."

"Zane, nobody would have to pay me to kill your ass, you sonofabitch. You're just another varmint taking up room in my town."

"Make your play, Billy Jim. Or crawl back in your hole."

"Zane, you're a dead man."

Colfax opened up with the Greener. He triggered two quick shots, aiming right where Zane stood behind the wall between the storeroom and showroom.

The twin explosions made a huge sound in the empty room.

Seneca whimpered behind Lew and put her hands to her ears.

In that instant, Lew knew what he had to do. And he knew he had to do it fast.

6

Two loads of double-ought buckshot ripped into the back wall of the store. To Lew, it sounded like the entire wall was going to collapse and fall on him. Splinters of wood leaped into the air. The wall groaned. None of the shot penetrated all the way through, but shot came through the opening and splattered the back of the storeroom, sounding like hail as it pinged off metal objects.

Colfax dropped the shotgun and went for his pistol.

Lew stepped out from behind the shattered wall, thumbed back the hammer on his Colt, and leveled it at Colfax. The pistol exploded and kicked upward. Lew brought it back down, hammered back, and sent another slug straight at Colfax. With the lamplight at his back, it was difficult for him to see. He hammered back again, ready to shoot if Colfax's pistol cleared its holster.

Colfax took the bullet low on his hip. The

force of the projectile spun him around in a half circle. He jerked his pistol from its holster in a purely reflexive action, cocking it on the draw. He went into a crouch and fired at Lew as he attempted to recover and find solid footing for legs that were already going weak from shock and loss of blood. The roar of his pistol boomed through the showroom. Billows of smoke rose from both pistols and hung in the air like a ghostly pall in the half-light.

Colfax fired again, but his aim was not true, and the bullet went wild, smashing into a shelf full of tin flashing, the ricochet bursting open a keg of tenpenny nails that rattled on the floor like metallic rain. Lew hammered back and fired another round at Colfax, but the sheriff had moved and the bullet whistled past him and struck the store window, shattering it to a jumble of tinkling shards.

Again, Colfax fired, but he was moving to a dark corner, shooting on the run, and his bullet plowed a furrow in the floor six inches from Lew's foot, sending splinters into his right shin. Lew fired again at the running man, but failed to lead him far enough. The bullet whined out of the store through the shattered window and caromed off a bell across the street with a loud *thwong* that quickly died away in the torrent of rainfall.

Colfax reached the corner, braced himself, and held his pistol up with two hands, trying to get a bead on Lew. Lew strode deeper into the darkness off to his right, fired another round at the place where he thought Colfax would be. He had an afterimage glowing in his head from the orange flash of Colfax's pistol, but the minute he fired, he knew that Colfax was no longer there. The bullet thudded into the slat side of a wooden wheelbarrow and mushroomed into a lead pellet that fell, spent and mashed, onto to the lid of a paint can.

Seneca, her knees quivering, her legs shaking, dropped to the floor and crawled over to the desk. She pulled the chair away and crawled underneath into that cramped space. She drew her knees up to her chin until she was in the shape of a ball. She continued to tremble, her eardrums vibrating with the sound of the explosions.

Lew crouched down behind the skeletal frame of a moldboard plow, his eyes narrowed to slits. He stared at the corner where Colfax had gone, looking for any sign of movement. He waited for the next flash from the sheriff's gun, his finger tight on the trigger, squeezing it just enough to take out the slack. There wasn't much. He knew he had a trigger pull of less than three pounds.

But Colfax didn't fire his pistol. Nor did he move.

Both men seemed to freeze in the shadows, neither willing to make the first move. The seconds crawled by. The silence grew like a massive presence in the darkness, amid the din of rain and wind. The pelting rain muffled all sounds of breathing. Each man, and Seneca, could feel the boards in the walls reverberate from the sound of the rain drumming on the shingled roof, a relentless pounding that echoed in the chamber of the showroom.

Sweat beaded up on Lew's forehead. His palms began to moisten, and he had an itch over his left eyebrow that he did not dare to scratch. There was madness in that empty room now, a madness born of the incessant patter of raindrops on the roof, the outside walls. Each person became aware of the wind. It blew through the shattered front windows, streamed along the floor in a chilling updraft, and whistled over plows and wheelbarrows, rattled the hanging hoes and rakes and shovels, whispered in every crack and cranny of the store.

The silence existed only between the two men at opposite ends of the room. It was a

61

silence of cunning, of murderous thoughts, of anticipation. Lew drew a breath and eased up the pressure on his trigger finger. It was growing numb. He let his breath out slow and flexed his finger, just for a second. Or two. Then he eased his finger back onto the trigger, took up the slack, and waited some more.

Neither man spoke, and that terrible silence between them grew to monstrous proportions. To Lew, it was like being in a dark cave with an animal he could not see, a ferocious animal that was stalking him as silently as a wraith. His ears strained to hear even the faintest sound from that corner where Colfax had gone, a breath, the scrape of a boot, the creak of leather. Anything. The silence got hard as granite. It sat there like an immense boulder that neither man could see through, or move out of the way.

Moments passed. Agonizing moments that taxed the patience of both men, that strained their nerves taut, to the breaking point. The silence grew larger, harder, more impenetrable, despite the monotonous mutter of the rain on the roof, the clatter of water in the drain spouts, the swish of its broom across the floor where the wind blew in through gutted glass windows.

The wind abated for a moment.

That's when Colfax opened up.

He fired two quick shots, fanning his six-gun with a rapid slap of his hand on the hammer. Two flames erupted from the corner, orange flashes that briefly illuminated the sheriff's crouching form. Lew fired in between bursts, holding low, just beneath the first blossom of exploding powder. He heard the bullet strike something soft. Then he heard a grunt, followed by the sound of a body slamming into something wooden, perhaps the corner of the wall. There was a low groan coming from that same corner.

"Zane, you bastard," Colfax growled, his voice laden with the gravel of pain.

Lew moved to his left, careful where he stepped. He eased the hammer back on his Colt, but did not fire.

Another low groan from the corner. Then, the metallic click of a cocking hammer.

But no shot.

Lew waited, his nerves singing like banjo strings plucked with an iron chisel.

More groaning. Soft, low. Muttered curses.

Did Colfax have something up his sleeve? Was he going to fire off another shot?

A man thinks strange thoughts at such times. Hunkered down as he was, Lew tried to picture where his bullet had gone, the damage it might have done. Was Colfax leaning against the wall, or had he gone down? Was he crumpled up into a ball, his life leaking away with every pump of his heart?

Lew did not know.

The wind slashed at the openings in the broken windows, hurling rain like silver lances into the store. The intensity of the rain increased, sounding like a billion rim shots on a snare drum. The wind howled, shrieking like some wounded ghost, keening against the sharp edges of the building, the ceiling inside.

"Zane?"

Lew didn't answer. He shifted his grip on the pistol, held it high, near his shoulder, his arm extended almost full length. He marked the sound of Colfax's voice, tried to picture his target in his mind.

But he did not shoot, either. He waited.

"Zane. I'm done for. You bastard."

It could be a trick, Lew thought. Colfax might want to draw him out in the open and fire that bullet tucked away in the cylinder in the hammer's direct path.

"Should have killed you a month ago," Colfax said.

Colfax's voice had grown weaker. The last

64

words came with breathy emphasis, spread wide apart, spoken slow, with effort.

Was the sheriff bleeding to death? Was he playing possum?

Lew didn't know. He just knew that he didn't trust this man with a badge, a man as corrupt as Pope and Canby, a traitor to his profession as an officer of the law.

Lew extended himself and stretched out flat on the floor. He began to slide out into the empty aisle. The rain covered the sound of his clothes scraping on the wooden floor. He inched along until he was onto the wet part. This made it easier for him to wriggle in between objects that were stacked along the aisle: milk cans, coils of manila rope, nail kegs, paint cans.

"Zane?" Colfax called out again. His voice was even weaker than before.

And he was very close to where Zane had crawled.

"You ain't gonna answer, are you?"

In his mind, Zane said, "No."

He crawled closer until he could hear Colfax's heavy breathing. He strained to pick out the blob that was Colfax from the heavy shadow in the corner. He thought he saw something, but he couldn't be sure.

"Get me a doc, Zane. For God's sake, show some mercy, will you?"

Zane thought about that. It was a reasonable request for a dying man.

"Slide your Colt toward the front door, Colfax," Zane said, raising his head some distance off the floor.

A mistake.

Colfax fired his pistol, as Zane hugged the floor. The bullet steamed over Lew's head. He saw the flash, the outline of Colfax. The sheriff was propped up in the corner, sitting, his clothing soaked with blood. Lew knew right where Colfax was.

Lew got to his feet in an instant. Crouching, he took aim on the place where Colfax sat. He squeezed the trigger and stood up. He ran to the corner and fired another round into Colfax, just to make sure. He looked down, saw the pistol in the sheriff's slack hand. He kicked it away and bent down close, cocking his pistol. He put the barrel against Billy Jim's forehead, wondering if he still had a live cartridge in the cylinder.

Colfax made a rattling sound in his throat. He wheezed a last breath and keeled over. Lew touched two fingers to the carotid artery in his neck, feeling for a telltale pulse.

Colfax was stone dead.

Lew squatted there next to Colfax, listening to the rain. Spray splashed against his face. The sound was suddenly soothing and he felt strangely calm for having just killed another man.

After a few moments, he heard Seneca call out to him.

"Lew? Lew? Are you still alive?"

He smiled in the darkness, took a deep breath.

He had never felt more alive in his life.

7

Lew stood up.

"Yes, Seneca," he yelled. "It's all over. I'm coming back."

He heard a scream of delight from the back room. He walked along the broken front of the store, the rain pelting him. He was impervious to it. It felt like a cleansing rain to him, a rain that was washing all the ugliness out of the world.

He walked up the aisle. A flash of lightning illuminated the entire showroom for an instant. He headed toward the light from the lamp on the office desk.

Seneca crawled out from under the desk when he entered the room. Her face was pale, her hair tousled, her clothes disheveled. Her cotton dress was wrinkled. She stood up and patted the unruly folds, pulled on the hem to straighten it.

"You're all right." She sighed.

"Yes."

"Is — did you . . . ? I recognized that voice. It was Sheriff Billy Jim, wasn't it?"

"Yes. He's dead."

She collapsed in his arms. He holstered his pistol and put his arms around her.

"They — they were all trying to kill you, Lew. Why are there such people in the world?"

"I don't know."

"Is it over? Is it really over?"

"I don't know that, either, Seneca."

She pulled away from him and looked into his face for a long time, as if trying to read his thoughts, as if trying to see if anything had changed.

"You look the same," she said. "But . . ."

"But what?"

"I — I don't know. All this. The killing. The blood. The kidnapping."

"Pope and Canby had no right to go after you to get me," he said.

"I know. I keep asking myself why they did it. Why they dragged me into . . ."

"Into my ugly mess?"

"Well, yes. I guess so."

"Is that all you care about? Getting your hands dirty over something I did?"

His jaw hardened and the lamplight flickered in his eyes and there were shadows there, too, and shadows of worry on his face that she hadn't seen before.

"I wouldn't put it that way," she said, the whipcrack of a retort in her voice.

"How would you put it, Seneca?"

"You're twisting my words, Lew."

"Untwist them, then."

She touched his arm, stroked the corded muscle under his wet shirt.

"I want to go home," she said. "Will you take me home, Lew?"

"Meet me out back. I'll fetch our horses."

They walked to the back room, past the bodies of Pope and Canby. She tried to avoid looking at the bodies, but curiosity overcame her and she looked at each one just before Lew stepped outside into the rain and the darkness. She shuddered.

"See if you can find us a couple of slickers, Seneca," he said, then went out the back door.

When he returned, riding Ruben and leading Seneca's horse, she had on a raincoat and held another in her hand.

"Come on," he yelled above the patter of rain. She came down the steps, handed him a raincoat, and went to her horse. She climbed into the wet saddle while Lew donned the slicker she had brought him. It was a little small so he didn't button it. But it kept some of the rain off his back.

Lew handed her the reins after she was in the saddle. She nodded to him.

Just as they were turning their horses, an angry woman appeared in the doorway, her stocky body silhouetted in the light.

"You — you murderers," she shouted. "Come back here. You come back here now."

"Who's that?" Seneca asked.

"Sarah Canby. Let's go. She's got Luke's shotgun in her hands."

They rode off fast, expecting to hear a shotgun blast, but there was only the sound of the relentless rain.

Lew headed for the road to Osage, Seneca following behind him.

He was sorry things had turned out the way they had. He knew he had turned still another corner in his life. He was sorry that Seneca didn't understand that he had been forced to kill those men. Perhaps she would understand someday, but for now, there was a gulf between them. She was probably still in shock, still confused by all that had happened. Still, he would have expected her to show greater courage, perhaps some compassion for him. Maybe, he thought, she doesn't know that I have to leave the county, leave everything I love behind. Including her. He would be a wanted man now, and he had already found that he could not expect any justice in the county, maybe not even in Arkansas.

Lew left Seneca at the bridge.

"You'd better go over to see Sheriff Swanson," he said.

"You're not going to ride home with me?"

"No. I'm a wanted man now, Seneca."

"But . . . I mean, you acted in self-defense."

"Do you really think Carroll County's going to look at it that way? I killed the Alpena sheriff, you know."

"I could be a witness."

"Not now, Seneca. I've made up my mind. Ed's probably still at Swanson's office. If not, Don can ride you home."

"You're just going to leave me like this?"

"Yes."

"You've changed, Lew," she said, her bitterness evident in her voice. "You've become . . ."

"What, Seneca? What do you think I've become?"

He could barely see her face, but he could feel her eyes boring into him. They were two shadows in the rain, faceless people, staring across a great distance at one another, neither seeing the other, but knowing that the distance was growing.

"I — I don't know," she said. "Maybe . . . maybe killing those . . . those men did something to you."

"Maybe my killing them did something to *you,* Seneca."

"Oh, so now you're putting it on me," she snapped.

"Putting what on you?"

"What happened up there in Alpena. You think it's my fault you had to shoot those men."

"No, I don't blame you at all. That would be stupid."

"But I was the reason you came after them."

"Maybe I was looking for a reason," he said. He knew he was being cruel, but he couldn't help himself. Seneca was plagued with doubts about him anyway. If it was going to end, whatever there was between them, then perhaps it was best to break it off now, before he left. He couldn't expect her to wait for him. He knew he would never be back.

"Well, maybe you were," she said.

"Good-bye, Seneca," he said. He touched two fingers to the brim of his hat and turned his horse.

She did not say good-bye, but as he rode away, he knew she was still there, watching him. He heard the sound of her horse's hooves on the bridge, riding away from him, riding toward Osage in the darkness and the rain. He choked back tears of self-pity and drew himself up straight in the saddle. He breathed in air to fill his lungs. But he could not fill the emptiness inside him, nor quell the swirling sickness in his stomach.

Damn it, he told himself, why hadn't he told Seneca that he loved her? He did love her. But they had both crossed a bridge and were heading in different directions. There was no use in flogging a dead horse. It was over. All of it. Only memories and sadness remained.

Lew did not spend much time at his house. He wrote a short note to his lawyer in Berryville, a man named Eugene Anderecky, wrapped the note, some bills as payment, and all the papers the Butterfields had signed, put them in an envelope, which he wrapped in oilcloth. He took some food he could eat along the way, got cartridges for his rifle and pistol, extra dry clothing and the money he got for the sale of his property.

He packed his saddlebags full, filled two canteens, and then rode off. He would take the back road to Berryville, drop the packet of documents off at Anderecky's house, then head north into Missouri. Once he was across the state line, he would head west. In a few days, he would be in Oklahoma and then decide where he was going.

For a time, he knew, men would be hunting him. They would probably make up dodgers and mail them to places he might go. If he was lucky, all that would take time, and he would escape capture.

He wondered what Seneca would tell her father. What she would tell Don Swanson. Don would have no choice but to ride up to Alpena to confirm the deaths and await orders from officials in Green Forest and Berryville. Then Swanson would be one of the hunters trying to figure out where he had gone.

Lew rode almost to Carrolton, then took the Green Forest road. He passed through Green Forest and went to Berryville, where he dropped off the papers at Anderecky's office, near the courthouse on the town square. He slipped the packet through a slot in Eugene's door. The rain continued and he saw no one. Nor did he see any lights, either in town or on the farms he passed.

It was still dark when he crossed the border into Missouri, and he crossed a river, going by dead reckoning. He did not know the country and there were no visible stars to guide him. He was, for all practical purposes, lost. He tried to think of Missouri towns he might know, but the only one he could summon to memory was Joplin, which he knew was fairly close to the Oklahoma border. If he could find a sign that said Joplin, he would follow such a road.

For now, though, he wandered in the dark, and he had no compass.

The rain stopped shortly before dawn, but the sky stayed dark and he heard the rumble of thunder far to the south of him. He came to what looked to him like a well-traveled road, and turned Ruben to the left, figuring it led westward if he had kept his bearings straight. He was sure that he had.

He passed a number of farms, where the smell of wet grain was strong in his nostrils. The road was muddy and the going was slow. There were places where water had washed across the road, cleaning off all the pebbles. He saw no tracks at that hour.

The sky lightened and he came to a fork where there stood a sign in the form of two white arrows painted with black lettering. He stopped to read it. One arrow pointed in the direction he had come from and said: SPRINGFIELD, 25 MILES. The other said: JOPLIN, 50 MILES.

Lew let out a sigh of relief.

At least he was on the right road and heading in the right direction.

A light wind came up and he took off his slicker. His clothes began to dry, and as the sun rose behind him, he felt the first chill as the ground gave up its cold. The wind began to warm. He stopped to give Ruben a hatful of grain at a creek and let him drink.

He looked beyond the bridge he would cross and saw the road stretch to the horizon. He heard cows lowing in a nearby pasture, and a pair of mourning doves whistled overhead, their bellies colored peach by the sun. He was not used to such flatness as he saw around him. Suddenly, he was homesick for the green hills he had left behind.

He knew he could never live in such a place, where the land was unbroken, the trees scarce, the creeks puny.

He knew at that moment where he was going to go, even though he had no specific destination in mind. He would ride west to the Rocky Mountains, leave behind the monotony of the plains.

He knew that it was a long way and that it would take him a long time to get there. He knew it was just the kind of place he wanted to be. It would be a place that reminded him of the Ozarks, with hills and hollows and long valleys, and streams leaping with fish, game aplenty in the woods.

He knew there must be such a place out West. There had to be. His heart demanded it.

8

The case was a week old by the time Horatio Blackhawk got to Alpena and interviewed Sarah Canby.

"You're a U.S. marshal?" she asked, staring at Blackhawk's badge.

"Yes'm. I rode down from Missouri, had orders from Kansas City. Judge Wyman over in Berryville sent a telegraph to my supervisor and he sent me down to investigate the murder of a law officer named Billy Jim Colfax. I understand you were an eyewitness."

"Wasn't only Billy Jim got murdered," she said. Sarah was still fixing up the hardware store, finding small pieces of glass in the flooring. The windows had been put back in, and the door fixed, but she had been unable to scrub away all the blood. And she was still finding shards of glass along the baseboards beneath the front window. She and Blackhawk stood there by the front window, with sunlight streaming in, high-lighting motes of dust dancing like silver fireflies in the air the broom had stirred up moments before.

"I understand, ma'am. Your husband, ah, Mr. Lucas Canby, was also killed."

"Murdered."

"Yes'm."

"Look over in the corner there," she said.

Blackhawk looked at the dark stain. He could still smell the lingering odor of bleach.

"Looks like you tried to get rid of some blood there."

"That's where that Zane boy shot Sheriff Colfax. There's bullet holes all over the place, I declare."

"Yes'm. Now, you saw this Zane fellow shoot Sheriff Colfax?"

"He shot him all right. I got here just after Sheriff Colfax died. His body was still warm. I saw that Zane boy and his galfriend making their getaway out back. It was him all right. Lordie, three men dead as God is my witness, and that no-good boy done it."

"Did you hear the shots?"

"It was raining cats and dogs, Mr. Black-hawk. You couldn't rightly hear yourself think. But I come down to the store to bring Luke and Virgil their supper. All these wind-ers was shot out and blood running ever'where in the front of my store. I didn't see Luke right off, but I went back and saw Virg a-lyin' there gape-mouthed, dead as a doornail, and heard them two out back and saw 'em ride off with me yellin' at 'em to come back, and then I seen Luke and I just broke into pieces."

"Yes'm," Blackhawk said. "I'm real sorry."

"You say you come down from Kansas City?"

"Well, I got my orders out of Kansas City. Telegraph caught up with me in Springfield."

"Up in Missouri?"

"Yes'm."

"How come not from Little Rock?"

"I was the closest. I'm federal, ma'am. Office wanted me to look into it since a law officer was killed."

"What about my Luke? And Virgil Pope?"

"I'm looking into those deaths, too, Mrs. Canby."

"Well, that gal knows something."

"What girl is that, Mrs. Canby?"

Blackhawk was not taking any notes, which made Sarah Canby eye him with suspicion.

"Why, that gal what was with Zane."

"What was the girl doing here?"

"You'll have to ask her."

"A lawyer over in Berryville said the girl's name was Seneca Jones and that she was kidnapped by your husband and Virgil Pope. He said that Mr. Lew Wetzel Zane had come up to Alpena here to rescue Miss Jones."

"Why, that lyin' booger. What lawyer was that?"

"Mr. Eugene Anderecky. Said that Zane dropped some papers off at his house and showed me the note Mr. Zane left among some other papers."

"He's a-lyin'. My husband didn't kidnap nobody."

"Thank you, Mrs. Canby. I'll ask Miss Jones about it."

"She'll lie, too."

"Yes'm."

Blackhawk left the store after bidding the angry Sarah Canby good-bye, and rode toward Osage, some thirteen miles south of Alpena. He was glad he had been sent here. His father had fought for the Union during the war, had been stationed in Springfield, was at the Battle of Pea Ridge, where he had lost his life. Blackhawk knew the bloody history of the border, but he liked the country, with its green hills, its lakes and streams. A peaceful place now, but during the war, the hills ran with blood, both

Union and Confederate. He had been too young to fight in it, but he was a keen student of history and had studied law in Columbia, Missouri.

He joined the U.S. Marshals Service to support his aging mother, widowed so young and crippled now with arthritis, and had learned to track and hunt men from a man who had worked out of Judge Parker's court in Ft. Smith, Arkansas, an Indian fighter he admired and respected, one Jesse Bodine, who had scouted for the Union Army.

A little over an hour later, Blackhawk was sitting in Sheriff Don Swanson's office, smoking a cheroot, his feet up on a chair. Don was smoking one, too, given him by Blackhawk.

"Haven't smoked one of these since I was a kid," Swanson said. "My pa used to have a hankering for them, until they got too dear."

"Nothing like a good smoke," Blackhawk said.

"How can I help you, Marshal?"

"You can call me Horatio. Can I call you Don?"

"Sure."

"What can you tell me about this Lew Wetzel Zane?"

"A lot, I reckon. I've knowed him since he was a boy. Knowed his folks, too. You hear what happened to them?"

"I got some of it from Judge Wyman over in Berryville. He said Zane was a hellion, that he murdered two boys, the sons of, ah, Pope and Canby."

"Painted you a pretty black picture, did he?"

"Pretty black, Don, yes."

"Well, I can give you one with a little more color in it, maybe. And not because I knowed the boy, but because I know what really happened down here with those two boys Wiley Pope and Fritz Canby. Yes, sir, it's a lot different story than the one you'll get out of Berryville."

"I'm all ears, Don."

Swanson told Blackhawk the whole story, about the two boys killing Zane's parents, robbing them, and being seen by an eyewitness. He told the marshal how Colfax had refused to arrest the boys, and how the judge in Carroll County thwarted the entire process. He told of the murder of the eyewitness and how Zane had pleaded with the authorities in Alpena, Green Forest, and Berryville to serve justice on the two murderers.

"Finally, Zane was forced to kill both boys

84

in self-defense. Of course Virgil Pope and Luke Canby were furious. They vowed revenge. Then I heard from Ed Jones, the father of Seneca, how she had been kidnapped by Virgil and Luke. Zane, who was sweet on Miss Seneca, went up to the house that night just after Seneca was abducted, and I guess he rode up to Alpena to rescue her. Which, according to Ed Jones, was just what Pope and Canby wanted him to do. They planned to kill him."

"Are you sure about that, Don?"

Swanson shrugged. "That's the way I heard it from Ed Jones. I have no reason to doubt his word. He's always been an honest man."

"So Zane took the law into his own hands," Blackhawk said.

"Well, you gotta admit the law sorta let Lew down, Marshal."

Blackhawk didn't reply.

"I reckon I'd better talk to Miss Jones," he finally said. "If you'd be so kind as to give me directions to her house. She live in town here?"

"No, she and her pappy live out on what they call Possum Trot. I'll draw you a map."

"Much obliged," Blackhawk said.

Swanson got a piece of foolscap from his drawer, dipped a pen in an inkwell, and drew a crude map. He blew on the paper when he finished, then handed it to Blackhawk.

"You just take that first fork to the left after you leave here. Follow it out and look for them landmarks. You won't have no trouble. Want me to go along? Won't even need a map that way."

"No, I'd better do this on my own. Thanks, Don. Any idea where this Zane feller might have gone?"

"No idea, Marshal. He talked about leaving, but he never said where."

Swanson stood on the porch and watched Blackhawk ride off. He admired the tall horse the marshal rode. It reminded him of his own mount, a Missouri trotter, sixteen hands high, good bottom, long lean legs. Blackhawk's horse was a dark brown with three white stockings, a small blaze on its face, flax mane and tail. Pretty as one of those Currier & Ives pictures like they put on calendars.

Blackhawk found the road to the Jones place easily enough. He had passed no one on the road, and spent his time admiring the country, going over the information he had gotten up to that point. He had not yet begun to form a picture of Lew Wetzel Zane, but the man was certainly fighting for recognition. Perhaps the girlfriend could tell him enough to fill in the remaining gaps.

He rode the slope up to the house, thinking how smart the man was who had built such a place. From the front porch, whoever stood there had a commanding view of the hills all around, as well as a long time to see whoever was riding up the road. He was not surprised to see someone standing on the porch, a rifle resting in the crook of one arm, his finger inside the trigger guard.

"Afternoon," Blackhawk said. "I'm Horatio Blackhawk, United States Marshal."

"Ed Jones. I see your badge, Marshal. Light down and come on inside. Use the hitch rail if you like."

"Thank you, Mr. Jones."

"Seneca," Jones called as he turned toward the front door. "We got company. You decent?"

Blackhawk smiled. Polite folks in these hills, he thought. Right proper.

He wrapped his reins around the hitch rail and climbed the front steps. Ed leaned the rifle against one of the posts bordering the steps and held out his hand.

"Pleased to meet you, Marshal Blackhawk. You come about the kidnapping of my daughter, I reckon."

"I'd like to hear about it, sir."

The two went inside. Ed held the door open, closed it behind him.

Blackhawk stared at the young woman who stood in the center of the front room. She had an apron bunched up in her hands, hands that were red from washing in lye-soap water, he surmised. He was surprised at her beauty, the natural beauty of a young woman who wore no rouge or jewelry, had on a simple cotton dress. She stood there in bare feet, and those were comely, too, he thought. Her hair hung down in ringlets, framing an oval face that was still peppered with freckles around her straight, patrician nose.

"Ma'am," Blackhawk said, taking off his hat.

"This here's Marshal Blackhawk, Seneca. You want some tea, or Seneca can boil us some coffee right quick."

"Pleased to meet you, Marshal," Seneca said. The marshal was glad that she didn't curtsy, but stood there, looking at him with a bold look in her eyes.

"Pleased to meet you, Miss Jones. No, I won't stay, thanks, Mr. Jones. If you folks wouldn't mind, I'd like to hear what you have to say about what happened to you a week or so ago."

"You mean about the kidnapping," Seneca

said, waving Blackhawk to her father's large chair. She sat demurely on the divan. Her father sauntered over and sat beside her so that they both faced the marshal, like willing witnesses.

"Yes'm, if you wouldn't mind."

"Surely," Seneca said. "I'll let my daddy start it off, like it happened, and then I'll tell you what happened after those two men dragged me to Alpena in the dead of night."

Ed and his daughter told their respective stories. Seneca left nothing out, even telling Blackhawk how she had felt after Lew had killed three men.

"I'm afraid I wasn't very nice to him, seeing as he's left and all without really saying good-bye."

"You mean he didn't kiss you or promise to write you," Blackhawk said.

Seneca blushed. "He just said good-bye and left me on the bridge. Rode off home, I reckon."

"What did you think about him killing those men?"

"Well, it was self-defense. And he was trying to rescue me from Virg and Luke."

"But you think he might have gone too far? Killing them like that?"

Seneca squirmed and started to wring her hands.

"No, it wasn't that."

"What was it?"

"I — I just thought he was a mite too calm about it. My brains were plumb rattled. All that shooting and the noise, the sound of bullets whizzing everywhere, hitting things in the store. It was like a nightmare, Marshal."

"I see."

"Maybe he just kept it all inside. Lew's that way. He doesn't say much sometimes, but I know he's thinking deep."

"Do you have any idea where he went, Miss Jones?"

She shook her head. "Out West, I guess."

"He ever talk about that?"

"No, not really. I just know his daddy took him elk hunting out to Colorado one year. Least, I think that's where it was."

"Thank you. Thank you both."

"What are you going to do, Marshal?" Ed asked. "You know that boy's innocent of any crime. It was self-defense, both when he killed those boys and their no-account fathers."

"And what about Sheriff Colfax?" Blackhawk said. "A man who had a duty to perform, who was gunned down in the performance of that duty."

"He was just as crooked as Pope and

90

Canby," Jones said. "Fact is, he was in cahoots with them, the way I hear it."

Blackhawk said nothing. Instead, he stared at Seneca for a long time, wondering if she was going to come to Zane's defense regarding the Alpena sheriff who had been killed.

She stared right back at him, her lips quivering ever so slightly as if trying to form words that were locked deep inside her and refused to let her utter them.

9

Lew had been riding for almost a week, discovering muscles in his body that he did not know he had until they started throbbing after each long day in the saddle. He had stayed well away from the towns, avoiding them even if it meant an extra hour's ride. He crossed into Oklahoma and was surprised at how quickly the land changed. There were gently rolling hills as far as he could see, a green, undulating land dotted here and there with farms where cattle and horses grazed under a perfect blue sky.

He passed a few wagons and carts, waved, and continued on his way without having to answer any questions. Roads seemed to lead off the main road and go nowhere, but all showed signs of traffic. On one such road, he saw horse tracks coming from some distant nothing and then heading west. They caught Lew's attention because he realized that the horse was favoring its left foreleg.

He expected to come across a lame horse at any moment, or one that had played out and could no longer be ridden.

At dusk, he smelled something and Ruben's ears perked up, stiffened to twitching cones. Smoke, Lew realized. The wind was from the west, and that's where the smoke was drifting from, beyond one of those rolling hills that seemed to go on forever. Lew kept Ruben at a walk and loosened the Colt in its holster. He'd had no trouble, so far, but one never knew what lay ahead on an unknown trail.

When he topped the rise, Lew saw the campfire, off to the right, in a cluster of trees by a small creek. There, from the signs on the road, was the lame horse, stripped of saddle, blanket, and saddlebags, tied to a tree, its left foreleg cocked like a hunting dog's leg. The man was chopping wood with a small hatchet and feeding split faggots into the fire. The sky was a smear of orange and pink and purple, the sun just below the horizon, tingeing the long thin clouds that hung motionless above the sunken cauldron that had burned his face all afternoon.

Lew was going to ride on by, but the man straightened up and lifted an arm in a beckoning wave.

"Ho, stranger," the man called. "Come.

I'm goin' to fix some coffee here directly."

Lew hesitated.

The man wasn't wearing a side arm, and his rifle was still in its boot, attached to the saddle. His voice sounded friendly enough, and he was a small man who looked to be in his fifties or sixties. Coffee sounded good to Lew. He hadn't had a hot meal since leaving Osage, preferring to light no fires at night, and anxious to keep riding in the mornings. Lew's mouth filled with saliva. His throat was parched.

He turned his horse and headed for the trees, the cool and inviting stream. Companionship.

"You got a lame horse," Lew said as he rode up.

"Lookin' that way. Light down. My name's Jeff Stevens."

"Lew Zane." He swung out of the saddle. "I'll take a look at your horse, if you like."

"Sure. I don't know why he come up lame. Been favoring that right leg since a while after we left home this morning."

"He's not lame yet, Mr. Stevens, but he's heading that way."

"Hey, call me Jeff, please. I'll have that coffee cooking in no time."

Lew didn't unsaddle Ruben, but tied him

to a willow tree downstream from Jeff's horse.

Stevens was short, wiry, with a day's stubble on his chin. His face was wrinkled with age. He looked like he was fifty or sixty. His old felt hat was crumpled and worn, stained with years of sweat and dirt. He had bright brown eyes, with the firelight dancing in them as he leaned over and stuck a coffeepot snug against the flames. He wore simple, homespun clothes, a linsey-woolsey shirt, duck trousers, work boots that laced up with leather thongs. He reminded Lew of some of the people back home, those who worked at the stave factory or who helped Ed Jones when he went to making sorghum.

Lew walked over to the crippled horse, straddled its left leg, and lifted its hoof. He could see it well enough in the twilight. He felt around the shoe, tested it to see if it was loose. It was a fairly new shoe, hardly worn at all. He felt for pebbles, any small, sharp stones that could have become wedged in between the iron shoe and the soft foot.

"I checked for stones in that hoof," Stevens said.

"None that I can find. Still looking," Lew said.

He touched one spot, however, and the horse pulled its hoof, trying to get it away from Lew's hands. He probed again, with his finger, once the horse settled down.

"Easy, boy," Lew said.

He felt something, a hard little stub in the back of the foot, just under the heel, near the frog. He put his thumb and index finger on either side of it and pressed inward. The horse winced. A ripple coursed up its leg, exciting each muscle. Lew's fingers tightened around the object, and he pulled at it. The horse jerked its hoof away and Lew fell backward. But he had the object. He held it up to the firelight.

"Got it," he said. "A danged splinter in its hoof, right at the heel."

"Be damned," Stevens said, and walked over. He looked at the splinter, then took it from Lew's hand. There was a smear of blood on it.

"Must of got that when I rode past my gate. Had some old rotten boards lyin' out there in a pool of water and old Leroy here must have stepped plumb in it."

"Probably worked its way in there," Lew said. "You put some mud and moss on that, and you got your horse back, sound as a silver dollar."

"Reckon that would do it?"

"Unless you've got some medicant salve. Some mud from that creek and a little tree moss. Just tuck it all around the shoe. Horse will absorb what it needs to close that hole up so it won't fester."

"Much obliged, Lew. Thanks."

Lew could smell the coffee. They both heard the water starting to boil. Jeff got a handful of soft mud from just under the creek bank, while Lew scraped some moss from the north side of a small oak. He ground it all up between his hands, rubbing his palms together to create friction. When Jeff held out his hands, Lew sprinkled the moss over the mud, then kneaded it all in.

Together, they packed the fissure around the horse's shoe with the mixture. Then Lew pressed the shoe on tight, squeezing the mud into the flesh and the small hole left by the removal of the splinter.

"That ought to do," Lew said. "He might favor that foot for a while."

"If you don't got a cup, I brung two," Jeff said. "That coffee's burpin' like a frog with the hiccups."

"I've got a cup," Lew said, and walked over to fetch it from his saddlebag. When he returned to the campfire, Jeff had put more kindling on the flames and had set the coffeepot to one side to keep the liquid hot.

"Set down, find yourself a spot, Lew."

Lew squatted well away from the fire. The

heat of the day still lingered along that stretch of creek and he had gotten a sweat up working on the horse. Jeff filled Lew's tin cup as well as his own, squatted a few feet away from his newfound friend.

"Where you headed, Lew?"

"No place in particular. West."

"Just seeing the country, eh? Wish't I was younger. I'd do the same."

Lew did not say anything. If Stevens was prying, and he didn't think he was, he didn't want to tell him too much. Talk left tracks the same as feet.

"Me, I'm going to Coloraddy. Got a letter from my daughter out there and she's in a heap of trouble, I reckon. She be needin' me if she'n and her young'uns are going to make it through the winter."

"Sorry to hear that," Lew said, having no idea what kind of trouble the man's daughter was in, or why she needed her father to help her get through the winter.

"Carol's a good girl. She just married the wrong man. He's nothing but a crook. That whole Smith family was no damned good, and Wayne was the worst of all."

Lew sipped the hot coffee, savoring the faint taste and aroma of cinnamon, a trademark of the Arbuckle's brand. The sky darkened in the west, leaving shreds of dark clouds turning to ash before disappearing. The blue faded in the east and Venus winked on, pulsing like a lone diamond in the blackening sky.

"Wayne was the head sheriff over in Bolivar," Jeff said, still musing aloud. "He got in with the crooked judges and lawyers, got real greedy and loose with the law."

Lew's interest piqued at the mention of Wayne Smith's profession.

"You say your son-in-law was a sheriff?"

"Mean as a bulldog with the rabies. Only, Carol didn't see it. He lied to her, like he lied to everybody else."

"Lied about what?"

"About how he was shaking down the criminals and the public. We never found out anything until after Wayne took Carol and the kids and left in the dead of night. Then it all come out, like dirty laundry on a line."

Lew took another sip of coffee and sighed.

"What do you mean about shaking down the criminals and the public? And how did you find out about what he was doing?"

"Whenever Wayne arrested someone, he'd ask the criminal if he wanted to go to jail or prison. When he caught a burglar, which he did, he'd give the man a choice. Pay the judge, the lawyer, and him, and Wayne would let him out on bail so he could ply his trade. The burglar would keep robbing people and pay the lawyer, who paid the judge and Wayne. When the trial came up, the burglar was always found not guilty. But Wayne went a lot further than that. He made the bankers and the merchants pay him so they wouldn't get robbed. Anyone who didn't pay, got robbed. Pretty soon he had money coming in from a lot of folks. Then someone robbed the bank. Someone Wayne didn't know and couldn't catch. The banker raised Cain and told the newspapers and it all come out, everything that Wayne and the crooked lawyers and judges had done."

Lew let out a low whistle of surprise.

"By the time we all read of his schemes in the *Bolivar Register,* Wayne was long gone. With all the money."

"And your daughter didn't know about any of this?"

"Nope. I reckon not. I never knew where Wayne had taken her and them kids until I got that letter the other day. She still doesn't know what-all Wayne done, but she said he fell in with some bad men and just left them. I think he found himself another woman."

"Jeff, that's the saddest tale I ever heard.

Makes my own story seem like a nursery rhyme."

"You got a story like that?"

"No, nothing like that. But I've run up against a crooked lawman back home. More than once."

"What did you do?"

"I took the law into my own hands."

Stevens finished his coffee and reached for the pot to pour another cup. He offered it to Lew, but Lew shook his head.

"Might keep me awake, Jeff. You make it strong, and I've got some miles to go yet."

"If you're going my way, son, you're welcome to stay and try your luck with my vittles."

"I don't know," Lew said.

"Way I look at it, Lew, if there ain't no law where you live, you got to become the law yourself. Otherwise, you're just easy prey, like a mouse in a room full of cats."

"The law doesn't look at it that way."

"If the law is bad, like it was in Bolivar, the people have got to root it out. They threw every one of those judges and lawyers in jail. And now we got us a sheriff who's honest and upholds the law. That's how it should be."

"Yeah, you're right, Jeff." Lew set his cup down and stood up.

"Still bound to ride off on your own, eh? It'll be dark as pitch tonight with a new moon rising."

Lew hesitated.

"I don't always talk so much," Jeff said. "Honest."

Lew laughed and sat back down.

"You're a pretty good talker, Jeff," he said. "I reckon we could ride together for a ways. Until we got on each other's nerves. What have you got in the way of supper?"

Jeff cracked a smile.

"It'll right sure stick to your ribs, Lew. If there's one danged thing I can do well, it's cook vittles. And I got deer meat that's going to turn rancid less'n we eat it. I got turnips and greens, too. I sure couldn't eat it all by myself."

Lew drew in a breath. His stomach flexed with hunger and his mouth filled with saliva. He looked up at the night sky, at all the stars that had suddenly appeared. He threw another stick of wood on the fire. Sparks of gold flew up and danced on the air.

"I'll unsaddle my horse," Lew said. "I just hope you don't snore, Jeff."

"I hope you don't, neither," Jeff said, and Lew smiled.

Maybe, he thought, he had made a friend in a friendless world.

10

Horatio Blackhawk was still staring into the blue depths of Seneca's eyes when Ed cleared his throat, as if to break the spell that seemed to have sprung up between his daughter and the marshal.

"You mean to stay a while, Marshal?" Ed asked. "If so, you better let Seneca fix us some tea or put the coffee to boiling."

"No, I won't be much longer, Mr. Jones."

Still, Blackhawk did not break his stare. Nor did Seneca, who seemed to be locking the marshal into some kind of dare. Ed crossed and uncrossed his legs, not knowing what more to say. He looked at his daughter, hoping she would look at him. But she continued that steady stare into Blackhawk's eyes. It was like a child's game, to see who would look away first.

"I gather, Miss Seneca, that you saw a change in Zane that night of the killings," said Blackhawk. "And you didn't like what you saw."

"Just call me Seneca, please. I don't want to get used to being called 'Miss.' "

"Oh, then you think Lew Zane will come back here someday?"

"I don't know," she said.

"Ain't likely," Ed said, "less'n the law lets him."

"Daddy, you hush," Seneca said. Then, to Blackhawk, she said, "I don't know what Lew will do, Marshal. I think he should have stayed and seen things through."

"What about that question I asked you, Seneca? Did you think Zane changed that night, that maybe the killings didn't bother him all that much?"

She drew in a breath, let it out slow, as if trying to collect her thoughts.

"I don't know what was in Lew's mind. I was upset when I saw Pope lying there dead. And then I saw Canby. All that blood. I wondered how Lew could do all that by himself. But I do know that those men were trying to kill Lew and he was just defending himself."

"What about Sheriff Colfax? Did Zane have to kill him, too?"

"I heard what Billy Jim said to Lew, Marshal. He came in that store to kill Lew."

"You're sure."

"Yes. I'm sure."

Blackhawk paused for a moment. He looked at Ed, then back at Seneca.

"Did you know Zane was planning to leave Osage before the night you were kidnapped, Seneca?"

She frowned.

"He never told me about it, if he was," she said.

"I think the reason he rode up here that night was to tell you he was leaving. Maybe the next day. Did you know that, Mr. Jones?"

Ed shook his head. "I knew he come up to see Seneca. I don't believe he said why."

"But you didn't know he was leaving town?"

"Nope."

"What makes you think that, Marshal?" Seneca asked.

"I spoke to Edna and Twyman Butterfield on the way into town. They own that store Zane's parents had when they were alive, where they were murdered by the Pope and Canby boys. They said Zane deeded the store to them because he was going to leave Osage."

Seneca gasped.

"He left the store to them?"

"And all the stock and furnishings at his

home. Yes'm."

Seneca and her father exchanged glances.

Blackhawk stood up, as if to signal that the conversation was over.

"It looks like Zane didn't tell you much about his plans, Seneca. It looks to me like he planned on killing those men up in Alpena before he left town."

"I don't believe you," she said. "He went up there because I was kidnapped."

"That was his excuse, maybe."

"Look, Marshal," Ed cut in, "it seems to me you're jumping to a lot of conclusions here. Lew had no way of knowing Pope and Canby were going to take my daughter. They're the culprits. They were using Seneca as bait so's they could kill Lew."

"Maybe. But fact is, Zane took the law into his own hands. He should have reported the kidnapping to Sheriff Swanson and let him go after Pope and Canby."

"Swannie wouldn't have done a damned thing. I know. I told him about the kidnapping that very night. I told him Lew was on his way up there."

"And what did he say?" Blackhawk said.

"Don said he'd look into it. I wanted him to go up there right away, get my daughter, keep Lew out of trouble."

"Was Swanson willing to do that?"

"Not right then. He said Alpena was out of his jurisdiction. He said Billy Jim Colfax could handle it and he'd ride up there the next day and check with him."

"That sounds right to me, Mr. Jones."

"Well, it damned sure don't sound right to me. Hell, all Swannie would have found was a dead sheriff who was helping two kidnappers."

"It might look that way to you, Mr. Jones. But in my book, Zane's been acting like a one-man vigilance committee. A vigilante. Breaking the law."

Blackhawk started for the door. Seneca got up and so did her father.

"Are you going to arrest Lew?" she asked.

"I'm going to do my best to find him and bring him before the court. He's got to answer for his crimes."

"What crimes?" Ed asked.

"Murder," Blackhawk said.

"That's so unfair," Seneca said, her voice rising in pitch. "Lew was doing what the law wouldn't do."

"Unless he was duly sworn and had a badge, Seneca, he was breaking the law. We have laws against people acting like vigilantes. We can't have every Tom, Dick, and Harry go out and pretend to be lawmen. It's what the law calls anarchy. Zane broke the law. He's got to answer for it. I'm leaving now. Good day and thank you both for answering my questions."

Before either Ed or Seneca could say anything, Blackhawk was out the door and walking down the steps of the porch.

"You don't really know that boy," Ed called after Blackhawk had mounted his horse. "He's not a criminal."

"Good day, Mr. Jones," Blackhawk said. He touched a finger to the brim of his hat in a farewell salute. "Seneca. You take care, hear?"

She opened her mouth to speak, but Blackhawk had put spurs to his horse and was already out of earshot, his horse heading down the hill.

"I hope Lew gets as far away from that man as he can," she said, wrapping an arm around her father's waist.

"You're not mad at Lew anymore, honey?"

"I'm mad at him," she said. "For not taking me with him."

"But . . ."

"I know. I told you I was mad at him the night he left me at the bridge. In the rain. But after listening to Marshal Blackhawk and thinking about things, I'm not mad about that anymore."

"What were you so mad about that night?

That Lew shot those men? Killed them?"

She looked up at her father and smiled. The two of them stayed there until the sound of hoofbeats faded into silence. They turned and walked back inside the house. It was quiet and cool in the front room. There was a cross-breeze blowing through the front and back windows.

Ed sat in his chair, the one where Blackhawk had sat. Seneca sat on the couch, curled up, tucking her legs up off the floor.

"When I saw those dead men, Daddy, I just got sick to my stomach. I hated them for what they did to me. I knew why they did it, too, and that made me even madder. They took me so that they could kill Lew."

"But you got mad at Lew for fighting back in self-defense?"

"I guess I was thinking about how ugly it all was. I wanted Lew to be punished for what he did. He broke one of the Ten Commandments. I wanted him to show some sort of regret at what he had done, at what he had been forced to do."

"That's understandable, honey. I guess."

"Then, I wanted him to punish himself in some way. For what he had done. But . . ."

"But what?"

"But he acted as if nothing had happened. I know he was just trying to get me back home, get me away from all that death. At the time, I thought he should have, oh, I don't know, said a prayer, or taken his hat off, shown some respect for the dead."

"Did you talk to Lew about your feelings on the ride back to Osage?"

"No. I just sulked."

"And what about Lew? Did he try to talk to you?"

"No, he just rode off. We both fought the rain. We were wet and both probably mixed up about what happened. I thought he would ride me all the way home. Instead, he just left me on the bridge, saying you were probably at Swannie's."

"Well, I was. Lew was right."

"Then, he should have gone there with me. Oh, I was so mad."

"And now you're not mad at Lew anymore?"

She drew in air through her nostrils, set her feet down on the floor.

"Why didn't he tell me he was going to leave Osage? He knew it that night. He knew it before he came up to Alpena."

Ed shrugged. "I guess he was just waiting for the right moment."

Seneca dropped her head and began to cry. She put her hands over her face and then just let the tears come.

"Oh, Daddy, I miss him so much."

"I know. I know."

"Why did he have to leave like that?"

Seneca was on the verge of hysteria.

Ed sat there, shaking his head, unable to put his feelings into words.

He let her cry.

And every sob tore at him like a wildcat's claws.

Finally, she stopped and wiped her eyes with her sleeve.

"I love him, Daddy," she said.

"I know. I'm sorry he's hurt you so, darling."

"He hasn't hurt me. I hurt myself. What is it they say? 'True love never runs smooth'?"

"That's what they say."

"I know Lew loves me, too, Daddy."

"Yes. And I'm sure you will see him again one day."

She didn't answer because she wasn't sure she would ever see him again. She shuddered to think what would happen to him if Blackhawk caught up to him. Lew was already a criminal in the eyes of the law. What had Blackhawk called him? A vigilante? Well, maybe he was, but he had not chosen to kill anyone. The law had forced him to become a criminal. A vigilante.

Justice, she thought, was indeed blind.

And then she began to weep once more, not for herself, but for Lew Wetzel Zane.

11

Lew could not erase that last image of Seneca from his mind.

Her face emerged out of the darkness, wet with rain, sad and lonely, lost. A face etched in pain and sorrow. The face of a stranger, finally. A face fading from memory with each passing mile, replaced by other images of her in other times, happier times. Then, even those fleeting pictures began to dodge him at every turn of thought, blurring together in a dizzying rush so that he could not pin down a single one of them.

Jeff's horse started walking better the second day as the wound in its hoof began to heal, and by the third day, the gelding was putting its full weight on the injured hoof. Jeff was content to let Lew take the lead until they were well into Oklahoma Territory, when Lew's course became erratic. Jeff began to grumble under his breath until Lew asked him to speak up.

"If you've got something to say, Jeff, just say it out loud. I know you've got something stuck in your craw, but unless I know what it is, you won't ever be able to spit it out."

"Seems to me we been ridin' in circles a lot. You lost?"

"I don't know. You check our course by the stars every night. You tell me."

"That's what I can't figure out. Why do you wander us off the trail so much? Gets me all confused. I try to keep my directions straight in my mind, but the way we been goin', I just lose all track of where anything is until I see where that afternoon sun is every day."

"Don't you ever look at the ground, Jeff?"

"Sure, I look at the ground. Why?"

"Ever since we got into Oklahoma Territory, I've been seeing pony tracks. Unshod pony tracks. Sometimes I double back to see if any new ones have crossed our trail. Sometimes I see the tracks and go in the opposite direction just so we won't run into any hostile Indians."

"I never seen none."

"Well, I'll point them out to you, next time I see any."

"You think we're being follered?"

"Oh, we're being followed all right. Every day. Why do you think I let you sleep while

I stay awake and then get you up so I can get some sleep?"

"That's just common sense on the trail, I reckon."

"Especially this trail, which is hard enough to follow. I know people have come this way, but it's awful lonesome out here and it gives my skin the crawls when I think about there only being two of us, and maybe whole tribes of Indians watching where we go and what we do."

"You put it that way, I reckon my skin's got the crawls, too."

"Well, keep your eyes open, Jeff."

There were wagon tracks on the trail they were following. Lew figured they were at least a week old. He had reckoned there were three wagons, heading west. Never any sign of anyone heading east, which gave him pause more than once.

He was beginning to like Stevens more each day. The man was good company and he had shared some of his life with Lew. None of his story came out all at once, but gradually, Lew was getting a picture of the man and his circumstances. He was even getting to like and respect his daughter, Carol. But the tale of what happened to Jeff's wife before Carol left and got married nearly broke Lew's heart.

"Alma was the sweetest lady you ever saw," Jeff had said one night. "Hardworkin', not too religious, and nary a complaint in twenty-odd years of married life and workin' a hardscrabble farm, the war, and all."

"What happened to her? Is she still alive?" At the question, Jeff's facial muscles shifted beneath the skin, and sadness cast a shadow over his features.

"No, Alma's gone. Choked on a chicken bone one night at supper. Carol was about seventeen at the time. One minute we were just sitting there, enjoying Alma's chicken and dumplings, when Alma kind of coughed and her arms stretched way out. I heard a big wheeze and then a kind of gasping sound. Alma pointed to her throat and her eyes got real wide, like she was in a panic. Carol gave out an unholy screech and my blood turned cold as winter ice.

"I jumped up and started beating Alma on the back. Carol just sat there, her hands over her mouth, face white as a bedsheet. I couldn't dislodge that bone in Alma's throat and her lips started to turn blue. I lifted her out of her chair and Alma kept wheezing, trying to draw breath into her lungs. She convulsed and I held on, but after a time, she just slumped over. I put her down on the floor, on her back, and opened her mouth. I reached way down in her throat and thought I felt something. I wrestled with it and it just kept going deeper. Carol was screaming at her mother, telling her not to die, but Alma was plumb gone and I couldn't bring her back."

"How horrible," Lew said.

"It was horrible. I turned Alma over on her stomach and started whacking her on the back. All over. She just lay there all slumped and lifeless. Carol got up and shook her mother. We turned her over again and I tried to fish out that bone. It was stuck pretty good, but I could feel it crossways, way down in her throat."

"Then, what happened?" Lew asked "Did you get the bone out?"

"Never did. Alma was dead and I just went kind of to pieces. Carol was crying her little heart out and I was crying and I told her to fetch a doctor. He came and pronounced Alma dead, and took her to the undertaker's. Far as I know, that chicken bone is still stuck in Alma's throat. Carol upped and married Wayne Smith pretty soon after that. I reckon she just couldn't stand to be in that empty house, what with me moping around and all, bawling all the time when I got to thinking of poor Alma."

Lew had said nothing and Jeff was quiet

the rest of the evening. Lew walked off by himself and looked up at the stars for a long time. When he got back to the campfire, where Jeff sat, Jeff's eyes were rimmed red as if someone had rubbed shaven onions in them.

The two men did not talk about Alma again, but Jeff talked about Carol so often that Lew began to think that he almost knew Jeff's daughter.

One day, Jeff asked Lew a question that startled him.

"Want to read that last letter I got from Carol?"

"I don't know. Likely, it's private."

"It is, but I been tellin' you about that daughter of mine and I thought you might like to see what she wrote. Can't never tell. You might meet up with her one day."

"I doubt if she'd like me reading her letter, being a stranger and such."

"Oh, you're not a stranger to me no more, Lew. Carol wouldn't mind. 'Sides, you can't never tell."

"Tell what?"

"Something might happen to me before we get to Colorado. I'm no spring chicken, you know."

"You're not that old and you seem to have your health, Jeff."

"Says you."

"Something wrong?"

"I feel my age. I feel time ticking away every livelong day out here."

"Maybe seeing your daughter again will cheer you up," Jeff said.

Jeff didn't reply. He just looked out in the distance and that sad look came over his face again. Lew had noticed that it was hard to wake Jeff some mornings, and when he did get up out of his bedroll, it took him a long time to get to his feet. Lew could hear the bones in his knees cracking and popping until the man had taken a few steps or flexed his legs.

They began to see other folks on the road, and for the past several days they had reined their horses off the road to let the Overland Stage pass them. The drivers never waved, just scowled at them, as did the shotgun men who sat beside them. None of the people on horseback or pulling wagons or carts spoke to them, either. They just eyed them with suspicion and hurried on by as if Jeff and Lew carried some communicable disease.

A couple of days after his conversation about Indians with Jeff, Lew halted his horse at the top of a rise. Before them stretched more road and more gently rolling terrain. A blue sky, pocked with a few puffs of clouds, gave him the feeling of being lost in the immensity of the country. But that was not why he stopped.

"What're you stoppin' for?" Jeff asked. "Not anywhere's near noon yet."

"You wanted to see tracks. Look down at the ground here."

Jeff looked down at the ground.

"I see a lot of tracks," he said.

"Pony tracks," Lew said. "Unshod."

"Yep."

"They milled around here, stopped. The way the tracks are facing, I'd say they were looking down the road. It's like a ribbon, a wavy ribbon."

"Uh-huh, disappears with each fold of the land."

"Chances are, the Indians saw something."

"How do you figure that?" Jeff asked.

Lew rode a few feet down the road. Jeff followed him.

"Here," Lew said, "they split up into two groups. Their tracks straddle the road."

"Funny. Maybe they don't like white man's roads."

"Look at the way the tracks drift off, one right, one left. They are going to follow this road, but stay out of sight of anyone on it."

"How do you know that?"

"Why else would they split up and widen the gap between their course and the road, yet keep the same heading?"

"Seems to me you're figuring a whole hell of a lot over some stray pony tracks."

"We'll see," Lew said. He loosened the Winchester in its scabbard.

They rode down the slope, following the road.

"You stay on the road, Jeff. I'm going to roam both sides, see if those tracks still hold. They're pretty fresh."

"Now you're giving me the crawls again, Lew."

Lew knew his hunch had been right when he saw that the tracks were heading west, but for a while he lost sight of Jeff, so he knew the Indians were trying to catch up to whatever was on the road without being seen.

Hills and more hills. Up and down.

Then Lew and Jeff, both following the road again, heard the sound. Off in the distance, ahead of them.

"What in the hell is that?" Jeff asked. "Sounds like a bunch of kids catcallin' at a swimmin' hole."

"I've never heard anything like it before," Lew said, "but it sounds like Indian war cries to me."

They listened. The high-pitched shrieks faded in and out of hearing.

"That popping sound," Jeff said. "Hear it?"

"Yeah."

"What is it?"

"Gunfire," Lew said. "Somebody's in trouble. Come on. Let's ride."

Lew ticked Ruben's flanks with his spurs and the horse bunched its muscles and bounded down the slope. Jeff followed, his horse gathering speed on the downward run.

As the two riders closed on the yelps, the war cries grew louder, and they heard rifle fire snapping like bullwhips. Down one hill and up the next, and still no sight of the conflict. Then up another long hill and at the top, they saw three wagons at the bottom. Near-naked Indians slashed in and out of range, their ponies like gazelles, swift and agile. Puffs of smoke belched from under the wagons, and from the rifles of the Indians. The Indians rode low on the sides of their ponies until they rose up, slightly, to fire their weapons.

Lew counted eight warriors. There was a man lying behind the wagons and he wasn't moving.

Lew had no idea how many people were

in or under the wagons, but they seemed to be outnumbered. He saw no Indians unhorsed, which was a tribute to their cunning, he thought.

When Lew and Jeff were close enough to get into the fight, Lew drew his rifle, cocked it. He wrapped the reins around his saddle horn and brought the Winchester to his shoulder. He picked out a lone Indian in the middle of a tight turn, led him just a hair, and squeezed the trigger. The brave rode into the bullet and flew off his horse as if he had been roped. He hit the ground and skidded as his pony completed the turn, then galloped off, away from all the shooting and noise.

Jeff fired his rifle, too, but the shot went wild.

The Indians noticed the two intruders and turned to give battle, three of them riding straight at Lew. He grabbed his reins with his left hand, jerked Ruben to a halt, and brought his rifle up to his shoulder again, while levering another cartridge into the firing chamber.

He sighted on the nearest charging Indian and led him a foot. He squeezed the trigger and the Indian's body jerked as the lead struck him in the chest. Blood squirted from the hole, but the warrior held on, somehow, and kept coming. But Lew knew the man was dying. Every beat of his heart was pumping out his lifeblood.

A woman screamed, and Lew saw two Indians drag her out from under one of the wagons. They disappeared behind the wagons and he couldn't get off a shot.

Two Indians charged at him from opposite directions.

Lew's blood froze. He could only shoot one, and then the other would have him dead in his sights.

Instantly, Lew made a decision, knowing his life, and perhaps Jeff's as well, hung in the balance like a man teetering on the edge of a high sheer cliff.

12

Lew had never seen an Indian that close before, as close as the nearest one was to him. He felt himself becoming almost hypnotized by the man's savage looks, his bare skin, the streaks of paint across his forehead and on his cheeks. The pony was eating up ground like a racehorse, and the warrior had his rifle at hip level, aimed straight at Lew. Out of the corner of his eye, Lew saw the other Indian closing in on him. They had him in a veritable pincer, out-flanked and outnumbered.

Lew took a trick from the Indians' book. He wheeled Ruben over hard, leaned back, brought his rifle down and aimed it, hip high, at the charging brave. He squeezed the trigger while his stomach tied itself into a knot, then kicked Ruben hard in the flanks to pull him out of the turn and head him straight at the other attacking Indian.

He didn't have time to see if his bullet

had struck home. He levered another cartridge into the chamber, heard the soft *whing* of the empty shell as it ejected. In a foolhardy tactic, Lew charged straight at the warrior on his right flank. This maneuver startled the Indian and caused him to crawl back atop the bare back of his pony so that he could turn his mount out of the way. Otherwise, he was going to be run over by a bigger horse and, perhaps, get unseated from his pony.

Lew saw the Indian jerk the rope halter of his pony, the muscles on his arm bulging and rippling with the effort. But the pony had no room to escape Lew's charge. It tried, but it was locked into a turn so tight it had to scramble to keep its footing. As the pony whirled hard over, Lew shifted his weight to the right side of his saddle, swung his rifle around, and aimed it at the warrior's back. When Ruben was galloping past the turning pony, Lew poked the rifle out from his waist and pulled the trigger. He fired at point-blank range, straight into the Indian's exposed back. The Indian jerked as if stricken with an electric shock and hunched over his pony's neck, blood spurting from a hole right next to his spine. The sight made Lew's stomach turn. He knew the Indian was mortally wounded and probably partially paralyzed. At the same time, he felt sorry for the pony as blood seeped down its side. The bullet had gone clear through the warrior and struck the pony. Its legs turned to rubber. It wobbled a few more feet, then crumpled to the ground. The brave fell off on his side, his eyes glazed over with the frost of death.

Lew cranked another cartridge out of the magazine and wheeled Ruben toward the wagons. He was bristling with action, his senses sharpened to a keen edge, his blood racing with fire, his heart pumping at the excitement. He was ready to do battle with whatever or whoever stood in his way. His nostrils flared as he gulped in oxygen, his mouth tightly shut, his face a grim mask of determination and anger.

Rifle fire crackled in his ears. He saw the Indians scatter, gallop away on their fleet ponies. Lew reined Ruben in and put his rifle to his shoulder. He fired another shot at one of them just before he disappeared over the crest of the next hill, and then everything grew quiet. He sat there in the saddle, still fuming, and glanced around, looking for Jeff.

Jeff rode up to him, sliding his rifle back in its sheath.

"Boy, you are some Indian fighter, Lew.

Lookie what you done. You run 'em off all by yourself."

"That's crazy, Jeff. We all ran them off. They just had enough, that's all."

"Take a look at them pilgrims over by the wagons. They're ready to give you your own parade."

Lew turned and glanced at the wagons. Two men were comforting the woman who had been dragged from under one of the wagons, and others were standing in a row staring at him, their clothes covered with dust, their eyes wide as a bug-eyed rabbit's.

"They're in shock," Lew said. "Let's go see if they need any help."

The two rode over to the wagons. Lew touched a finger to the brim of his hat in greeting. One man stepped out.

"Thanks, stranger," he said. "We were in a bad spot there."

Lew looked at the two men lying still on the ground.

"I'm sorry about those two," Lew said. "Anything we can do to help?"

"I'm Faron Briggs," the man said, walking up to Lew and lifting up his hand to shake Lew's. "We didn't see them Cherokees comin'. Kilt two of us before we could get off a shot."

"How about the woman?" Lew asked. "Is

she all right?"

"She'll be fine. Just scared is all."

"How do you know those Indians were of the Cherokee tribe?" Jeff asked.

"I been this way before," Briggs said. "Generally, the Cherokees just ask for some tobacco or money, sometimes a little whiskey or some trinkets. Then they go on their way. But these varmints just went plumb crazy. Started shootin' and hollerin', coming after the horses, tryin' to cut the traces and make off with them, I reckon. We kept up a hot fire, though, and they didn't get nothin'." He paused, then said, "I got to go see about the lady. Excuse me, gentlemen."

Briggs walked over as two men walked the woman back to one of the wagons. Her hair was disheveled, but she didn't seem to be badly hurt. Briggs spoke to them, then returned to where Lew and Jeff sat their horses.

"Be obliged if you could ride along with us," Briggs said. "We have two men to bury, and then we'll be on our way."

"Where you headed?" Jeff asked.

"Santa Fe. Where you going?"

"Colorado."

"You could ride with us, then. We'd feed you. The lady there makes good coffee."

"What do you think, Lew?" Jeff asked.

"Slow us down, considerable."

"Yeah, it might. No, thanks, Mr. Briggs, we got to be on our way."

"Some of the men want to go after those Cherokee," Briggs said. "They're hoppin' mad at what they done to us. You could maybe get you some scalps."

Lew shook his head. He didn't like the direction the conversation was taking. He wanted no part of hunting Indians and killing them, if it could be avoided. And he sure as hell didn't want any bloody scalps.

"We'll be on our way, Mr. Briggs," Lew said.

"What did you say your name was, feller?" Briggs asked, suddenly suspicious.

"I didn't say."

"You got something to hide? You on the run?"

"I have nothing to hide. I just don't give my name out to strangers."

"No need to get your dander up. Just curious."

"Have a safe trip, Mr. Briggs," Lew said. "Come on, Jeff. Let's go."

Jeff seemed reluctant to leave, but Lew was already riding away from the wagons. He waved a hand to the men and women watching him. They looked surprised to see him leaving. Jeff caught up with him, and when they were out of earshot of Briggs, he opened up with some questions.

"What did you want to rile that man for, Lew? How come you didn't want to ride a ways with them? They seemed like hospitable folks."

"If I thought we could have helped them, I would have stayed. But those folks were bent on revenge. They wanted blood."

"Can you blame them, Lew?"

"No. In a way I can't. But if they hunt down those Cherokee and kill any of them, who knows what will happen after that? They might bring the whole tribe swarming down on them."

"But they're in their rights to go after those Indians and kill ever' one of 'em."

"That's their decision."

"What? You don't think they're right?"

"I don't know. There was death on both sides. I killed a man or two. I don't feel good about it."

"But the Cherokees attacked first. They was in the wrong."

"And they paid a price."

"But they was Indians."

Lew prodded his horse with his spurs as if to ride away from the conversation. Jeff caught up with him a moment later.

"Let it go, Jeff," Lew said.

"Look, I'm just trying to find out who I'm ridin' with is all. I got a right to ask questions."

"You don't like riding with me, go on back and take up with Briggs and his bunch."

"Aw, it ain't that, Lew. I just wonder what you'd do the same thing happened to me. Would you just let it ride? Not try and take revenge?"

"Revenge is a thing I know something about, Jeff. It doesn't taste good. Revenge leaves a man empty inside."

"How would you know that?"

"I know," Lew said.

They rode on, into the sunset, not speaking anymore, and not seeing any more Indian sign. That night, they didn't make a campfire, and left the next morning without coffee or anything to eat. The country, with its endless vistas devoid of human life, seemed to swallow them up. With Lew silent as stone, Jeff ended up muttering to himself, speaking broken sentences that seemed to make no sense, either to him or to Lew. They chewed on hardtack and jerky and drank water to wash the dry food down. Late in the afternoon, Lew finally said something to Jeff.

"Will you stop grumbling to yourself, Jeff? There's plenty of good silence out here and

I want to enjoy it while it lasts."

"I wasn't grumbling none."

"Well, it sounds that way. We couldn't hear any ponies approaching us."

"You think them Cherokee are going to come after us?"

"No. I think they've got better things to do. But no need to invite trouble."

"I wasn't inviting anything." Jeff glowered at Lew, jutting out his chin as if begging Lew to take a swing at him.

"We need fresh meat," Lew said. "I'm thinking I ought to start shooting jackrabbits."

"Well, there's plenty of 'em."

"I'll get us one or two for supper. We'll build a fire tonight. Maybe have some coffee."

"Now, you're talkin'," Jeff said.

That night, Jeff let Lew read his daughter Carol's letter as they sat by the fire, their bellies full, hot coffee in their cups.

"She's a good girl," Jeff said. "Met the wrong man. But she's got spunk. Maybe you'll meet her one day. Here's her letter."

Jeff unfolded the letter he took from his pocket. The creases were beginning to wear, but Lew could read her handwriting, which was clean and neat.

The letter told of Carol's troubles with

her husband, how he had left her and the kids to fend for themselves. Lew could sense the bravery behind the words as she spoke of how she was managing to survive without any money. At the end, however, she sounded an ominous note.

We are living in a canyon a few miles from Leadville. This is a small mining town filled with rough men. I'm almost afraid to go there, but that's the only place I can buy food and such for the children. I have been sewing to make ends meet. It doesn't pay much. There's a man in town I don't like and he's come out here once or twice. I shoo him away, but I'm afraid he'll come out when he's drunk and cause trouble. I might have to shoot him.

"Who's this man?" Lew asked as he handed the letter back to Jeff.

"I don't know. It's a worry, though."

Lew sipped his coffee and thought about the woman with two children, all alone, with no money and no friends. His heart went out to her, but Jeff was right about her having spunk.

He didn't even know Carol, but he was beginning to like her. She seemed, just then, a lot closer to him than Seneca, and every time he thought of Seneca, something squeezed his heart and he felt a hollowness inside. Maybe he shouldn't have left Osage. Maybe he should have stayed and cleared his name.

But he knew that would have been impossible. He had wanted justice, but it was denied him, hidden away by those small minds who passed as champions of the law. Money made those judges and lawmen run, not ideals or morals. He was glad to be away from them all. All except Seneca, and he feared he would never see her again. And maybe, she was a part of that same system back home. Maybe she, like them, was blind in one eye and couldn't see out of the other.

Lew watched the fire die down after Jeff went to sleep. The call of a coyote made him feel even more lonesome. And when the notes died away, so did all of Lew's thoughts of home fade away, too.

13

Judge Ringgold Thaddeus Wyman glowered from behind his desk. He wasn't angry at anyone. A glower was permanently on his face, caused in part by his thick, heavy jowls, his protruding shelf of a forehead, his close-set porcine eyes, magnified by the thick lenses of his horn-rimmed spectacles. He was an imposing figure in any setting, but in his office, he loomed large over the room like some fleshy-lipped gargoyle.

Present in chambers, listening to Wyman's every word, were Berryville Sheriff Rudy Cooper and the prosecuting attorney, Michael Farris. Rudy was a thick-necked, chinless barrel of a man with ruddy cheekbones latticed with ruptured veins caused by a prodigious consumption of rotgut alcohol. His hairy arms protruded from sleeves cut too short to cover his wrists, and he chewed on the stub of a cigar that he never lit. Mike Farris was a slender, clean-cut young man with a razor-sharp mind and a disarming smile that beguiled many a hapless witness on the stand in court. He was never happier than when his nose was buried in a law book.

"Where in hell is that federal bastard?" Wyman roared, glancing up at the large Waterbury clock on the wall. "He said he'd be here at ten of the clock, by damn, and I hate a man who isn't as punctual as a midnight piss."

"Mr. Blackhawk had some swollen creeks to cross after that rain we had, Judge," Farris said. "It's just now ten o'clock."

Cooper shifted the cigar stub in his mouth from one side to the other. His dead eyes gave him the look of a basking lizard.

"Judy," the judge roared, "look out the damned window and see if you can see that marshal."

"There's a man riding this way, Judge. On a big old horse. That could be him."

"Coop, don't you light that damned cigar," Wyman said, as if he needed to lash out at someone, guilty or not guilty.

"I never light these see-gars, Judge. You know that. I just suck the juice outen 'em."

"Oh, shut up, Cooper. You haven't got the sense God gave to a bantie chicken."

"Yes, sir, Your Honor," Cooper said.

They waited.

Then they heard the clump of boots on the hardwood floors in the outer office. Then the rustle of skirts as Judy arose from her little desk.

"The judge is waiting for you, Mr. Blackhawk. You just go right on in."

The door opened and Horatio Blackhawk filled the frame. He ducked his head and entered the office.

"Close the door, Marshal," Judge Wyman said.

Blackhawk turned and pulled the door shut behind him.

"Take this chair over here, next to my desk," Wyman said. "Shake hands with Sheriff Cooper and the county prosecutor, Mike Farris."

Blackhawk shook their hands and sat down.

Sunlight streamed through the large window in the judge's office. This one faced north; the one behind him had a western exposure. Blackhawk had stirred up several bevies of dust motes, and these danced in the columnar shaft of light that focused on his chair so that he was the only one in the room caught in the glare.

Wyman pulled a large gold watch from his vest. He dangled it from his gold chain, then steadied it with a pudgy hand.

"Punctuality, Marshal Blackhawk. This court runs on punctuality. The world runs on punctuality."

Blackhawk said nothing. He stretched out his legs and tipped his hat back on his head as if he had all the time in he world.

"Well," the judge said, and slid the watch back into his vest pocket. "Let's get down to business, shall we?"

Still, Blackhawk said nothing.

"Marshal," Wyman said, "just what do you intend to do regarding this murderer Zane? Have you made any progress in your investigation?"

"Well, I suppose you could say that."

"What, sir? Say what?"

"That I've made some progress. I know more about Lew Wetzel Zane than anybody in this room."

The judge reared back in his chair.

"What is there to know? The man's a murderer. He killed a peace officer. He's murdered five people that we know of. Zane is a dangerous man, and a fugitive from justice."

"In your eyes, Judge, Zane is all that. But I've been getting a slightly different picture of the man."

"I don't care what your picture of the man

139

is, Marshal Blackhawk. I want to know what you're doing to bring that man before the bar. I want him standing in my court so that justice can be meted out."

"You have one thing nailed down, Judge Wyman. Zane is definitely a fugitive. On the run."

"So go catch him," Wyman said.

"If ordered to do so, I will. As it is, I've completed my investigation down here and all that remains is for me to return to Springfield, write my report, and wait for further orders."

"That's not exactly so, Marshal," Farris said. "Your superiors have assigned you to Judge Wyman's court. He'll be giving the orders until this case is settled."

Blackhawk cocked his head and looked at the judge. Wyman continued to glare at him, but there was now a smugness to him as evidenced by his pooched lips and his folded hands. He seemed to be looking down on Blackhawk from a great height, as if he were actually sitting on the bench and not at his cherrywood desk.

"That so, Judge?" Blackhawk said.

"Yes, that's so, Marshal. But we've got a little sweeter pot to make the assignment a mite more palatable to you."

"Oh? And what might that be?"

The judge looked at Cooper.

Cooper cleared his throat.

"Well, sir, I just come from Alpena this morning and the widows of Virgil Pope and Luke Canby have put up a reward for the capture of one Lew Wetzel Zane."

"Not a reward exactly, Coop," the judge said, waving a hand across the desk at eye level. "I'm thinking some of it could be used to pay the marshal's expenses while he hunts down this killer, Zane."

"I'm paid by the United States government," Blackhawk said.

"We think you deserve better compensation than the government offers, Marshal."

"I couldn't accept it."

"No? Since you are assigned to my court, that is my decision, not yours. I think you'll be pleased at the amount we have to work with. Mike, you cleared this with Mrs. Pope and Mrs. Canby, did you not?"

"I did," Farris said.

Blackhawk said nothing.

"Let's take a look at that satchel, Coop."

Sheriff Cooper reached down and lifted up a brown leather satchel, carried it over to the desk, and set it down in front of Judge Wyman. Wyman opened the satchel's clasp. He reached in and began to pile paper money on the table in neat stacks.

"That's the money we can use to achieve swift justice in this case, Horatio. May I call you Horatio? It amounts to twenty thousand dollars."

"In reward money," Blackhawk said.

"Reward money and incentive money. I want you to hunt down Zane and I want you to have the financial resources to do so."

"I'd like to see confirmation that I'll be working under the jurisdiction of your court, Judge."

"Of course," Wyman said.

He took a sheet of paper from his desk, handed it to Blackhawk.

"That good enough for you, Horatio?"

Blackhawk handed the paper back to Wyman.

"I'm at your service," he said.

Wyman smiled. It was the smile of an indulgent parent. It was also the smile of a skillful manipulator. He swept the money aside and placed the sheet of paper in the center of his desk.

"Good. Now, what are your plans, Horatio?"

Blackhawk tipped his hat back square on his head and sat up straight.

"I've got a good idea where Zane is headed. I've got one more person to see here in Berryville. Then I can provision and be on my way."

"Where, may I ask?" Wyman said.

"West. To Colorado."

The judge counted out some bills, stood up, carried them over to Blackhawk, and held them out.

"Here's one thousand dollars to get you started, Horatio. If you run short or need more, for any reason connected with your duties in this case, just send a telegram and we will send you what you need."

"That's a lot of money," Blackhawk said.

"And there's nineteen thousand more waiting for you whenever you need it. And you will bring Zane in. Dead or alive."

Blackhawk entered the outer office of Eugene Anderecky's law firm in Berryville. A petite older woman greeted him from behind her desk.

"Marshal Blackhawk?" she said.

"Yes. Is Mr. Anderecky in?"

"He's expecting you, sir. Right through that door."

Anderecky smiled when Blackhawk entered. The two men had met before, briefly, early in Blackhawk's investigation.

"I already know that you're working for Judge Wyman on the Zane matter," Anderecky said. "Law clerks are wonderful sources of information."

"Do you also know that he is probably misappropriating funds?"

"Sit down, Marshal, sit down. Tell me all you can."

Blackhawk told him about the twenty thousand dollars in reward money, a thousand of which was now in his pocket.

"Apparently, Ringgold has that discretion," Anderecky said.

"He's a law unto himself, isn't he?"

"Yes, he is." Anderecky smiled.

"I just have a couple of questions, Mr. Anderecky. Then, I'll be on my way."

"Go ahead."

"You told me that Lew Zane transferred his parents' store over to the Butterfields. Have you recorded the deed yet?"

"I have."

"Did Zane ask for proof of that transfer and that filing?"

"He did."

"And where will you send that proof, Mr. Anderecky?"

"You'd make a good prosecuting attorney, Marshal. But to answer your question, he did not ask me to send such proof anywhere. He asked me to hold the papers in my safe."

"Did he say he'd be back for them?"

144

"No, he did not. He said he might be away from these parts for quite a while."

"Did he indicate where he might be going?"

"I'm afraid not, Marshal, and even if he did, that would be part of a privileged conversation and not subject to any divulgence of said conversation on my part."

"So you have no idea where Lew Zane might have gone?"

"I didn't say that."

"But if you do, you won't tell me."

"That's right. Lew Zane is still my client, until he tells me otherwise."

"Thank you, Mr. Anderecky. If he does contact you, or if you're in communication with him, you might tell him that I'm on his trail. It will go easier for him if he surrenders to me, rather than to Judge Wyman."

"You don't trust Judge Wyman?"

"About as far as I could throw this building you're sitting in, sir."

Anderecky smiled. "If you do catch Lew, I hope you'll take him someplace where he can get a fair trial. He'll never get one in this county."

"I know."

"And Marshal . . ."

"Yes?"

"One thing to keep in mind. Lew Zane is innocent of those charges filed against him in Judge Wyman's court."

"Isn't every man innocent until proven guilty, Mr. Anderecky?"

"Not in Carroll County he isn't. Not in Judge Wyman's court."

One thing Blackhawk knew, when he left Anderecky's office.

An innocent fugitive was just as dangerous as a guilty one.

And Lew Wetzel Zane had already proven just how dangerous a man he was.

14

They lived off the land, Lew and Jeff, taking jackrabbits at first, then making meat with deer, before they saw their first antelope. The prairie seemed endless, and Jeff had never seen so much grass before, and never grass so high as when they reached the Colorado plains. Each day was a wonder to him as he viewed, for the first time, the majestic buttes and mesas that glowed red in the sunlight, looked like fleets of earthen ships when he squinted his eyes.

"Tastes a little like goat," Jeff said on that first night when they dined on a fresh-killed antelope.

"How do you know? You ever eat goat?"

"Once't," Jeff said. "My pap had a few goats and pigs and a milk cow. Pigs died out from some kind of hog disease and he didn't want to butcher our cow, so we ate a goat until we found something better."

"This tastes pretty good," Lew said, gnawing on a hind leg roasted over their campfire. "Not much like pork and less tasty then beef, gamier than deer meat. But not bad."

"Pfaw. It's like chewing leather."

"I suppose you ate leather, too, in your boyhood days."

"Don't get smart, Lew. You're mighty sassy these days."

"It's the country, Jeff. It fills you up. It's so big and I've never seen sunsets like these. Not in the Ozark hills. There, they are quick, as if the hills smother all the fire and just leave smoke in the sky. Out here, with nothing to break your sight, they seem to last forever, and they look like paintings that shift colors ever so slowly, living paintings brushed onto the sky by an unseen hand."

"Whoo, boy, you should have been a poet."

"Well, you see them, too, Jeff. Don't they quicken your heart? Make you look at the world in wonder?"

"They mean the end of another long day," Jeff said, and continued to gnaw on a chunk of pronghorn meat that was so hard to chew, it made his jaw ache.

"Just look at that moon hanging up there like a lantern, Jeff, shining down on us like silver showered from heaven."

"It's up there damned near ever' night, Lew."

"But I've never seen it so close before. In this pure night air. And the stars, look at 'em, so bright and near. Why, it feels like I could reach up and touch them."

"Moon's no closer tonight than it was the night before and if you think you can touch them stars, just reach on up and grab one, why don't you?"

"You always this sour on life?"

"I'm not sour on life, but all that stuff in the sky don't matter none to me. I got things on my mind. Heavy things."

"What things?" Lew asked.

"Carol. My daughter. I keep thinking of her all alone, with those kids, suffering, maybe in danger."

"Worry never did anyone any good, Jeff."

"I can't just let it go."

"Maybe that's what you should do, though. Let it go. When you get out there, see her, you can do something. Now, you can do nothing."

"I can worry."

Lew laughed.

Human nature. There was no getting around it. People followed the course they had set for themselves. Jeff was just being human. A father worrying about his daughter.

They saw other travelers along the trail, avoided them when they could. They saw wagons of every description, some headed west, others returning from somewhere, Santa Fe, Taos, perhaps, laden with goods. They saw riders, too, some leading packhorses and mules, others bound for the West with nothing but the clothes on their backs, the belongings in their saddlebags.

They saw no Indians, nor did Lew encounter any tracks of unshod ponies. They drifted on and off the trail, guided by the polestar at night, by the sun during the day.

Finally, the mountains loomed in the distance, a small dark mass that gradually grew larger until, finally, Lew and Jeff could see the snowcapped peaks, the dark masses beneath them like a gigantic backbone stretching as far as the eye could see.

In the waning days of summer, when their horses waded through shimmering watery mirages that vanished before their eyes, only to reappear again yards ahead of them, they saw the town of Pueblo emerge from the morning haze, and they rode toward it, wide-eyed with wonder, their blood quickening, their hearts pumping in anticipation. For the first time in days, Lew saw a smile on Jeff's face, and he sensed the man's impatience as the distance between them and the town shortened and they could make out the individual outlines of adobe buildings nestled at the muscular foot of the towering mountains.

"I never saw so many smokestacks before," Lew said. "Look at all that smoke. Wonder what they're making."

"Carol says they're smelting. Silver and such. She says she could smell the smoke night and day when she and Wayne Smith were there."

"Does she live there now?"

"No. Up in Leadville, remember? That's where I'm going. What about you?"

Lew thought about it. He had no plans. He didn't know anybody in Pueblo, or in Leadville, either, for that matter. He had become a drifter, a man without a home, almost without roots. For the first time in their journey, he began to think about the future. Where was he going? What was he going to do for a living?"

"I don't know," Lew said. "I guess I'll have to look for a job."

"First thing I'm going to do is get a hotel room. Then I'm going to get a shave and take a hot bath. I'll probably stay in Pueblo a couple of days, then head into the mountains for Leadville. I'd like for you to come with me, if you're willing."

"I'll give it some thought. That bath and haircut sounds good. So does a real bed."

Jeff laughed. They were both bearded and their clothes were caked with salt from sweating so much. They had become used to each other's smells. Until now. Jeff had a rank smell to him that Lew had finally noticed. And he knew he stank just as much.

"There's the Arkansas River," Jeff said. "Runs right through town."

Lew saw it glistening in the sunlight. They had thought about following it to Pueblo, but would have had to ride miles out of their way to find it, going by way of Bent's Fort, and running into pilgrims traveling from Dodge City, a town with a bad reputation. So they had come the hard way, avoiding, as Jeff told him, "a lot of unsavory folks from Kansas."

They put up at the Fountain Hotel, named for the creek that joined the Arkansas River. Like most of the buildings, it was made of adobe brick and only had two stories. But the rooms were cheap and they offered a hot bath for four bits, and a shave for the same amount. They boarded their horses in a nearby livery stable, El Rincon, which took up a corner of a nearly empty street, and was run by a Mexican named Jorge Gonzales. Gonzales, it turned out, knew a lot about Pueblo, and some of his information concerned recent arrivals of many of those same unsavory folks Jeff had spoken about on the trail. He knew quite a bit about Wayne, Carol's husband, as Jeff soon found out.

"Oh, yes, that one," Jorge said. "He works as a deputy sheriff, but the people, they complain about him."

"Why, what do they say about Wayne?" Jeff asked.

"That he steals money from them. He says it is for their protection, but they say it is for his pockets."

"Where might I run into this deputy sheriff?" Jeff asked.

"At night, he is at the Double Eagle Saloon. He has a girlfriend who works there. A woman named Flora. She is a bad one, they say. I do not know."

"Why is she bad?"

"She gets the men drunk and then these men are rolled when they leave the cantina, their pockets turned inside out. I think she and the deputy sheriff share in the profits from this occupation."

After they had bathed and gotten shaves, the two men ate at a restaurant called Rosita's, recommended to them by the clerk at the hotel. It was a two-block walk and the evening was cool. The clerk had told them they were a month away from their first snow.

At Rosita's, Lew asked Jeff about Gonzalez. "Why did you want to know about Carol's husband? You're not going to kill him, are you?"

"No. I just want to ask the bastard why he left my daughter up in Leadville and took up with this whore, Flora."

Lew stiffened in his chair. His knife and fork hovered above his steak.

"Do you want my opinion, Jeff?"

"Well, opinions are like assholes, Lew. Everybody has one."

"Some free advice, then."

"I'll listen."

"Stay away from Wayne Smith. And if you do see him, don't ask him why he abandoned your daughter. The man sounds like trouble. Big trouble."

"I just hate what he's done to my daughter. And I hate to know he's getting away with it."

"Whatever he's done, is done. You can't do anything about it. And if you stir up a hornet's nest, you're going to get stung."

"That's good advice, Lew. Well taken. I

guess maybe I just want him to see me, so he knows Carol is not alone."

"That's all right, then. We'll just go to the Double Eagle, have a drink, and let it go at that."

The Double Eagle was crowded. Men from the smelters packed against the bar, hardcases sat at tables with painted women, and drifters nursed drinks and smoked cigarettes, looking for handouts. Jeff and Lew made their way to the bar and waited in a line for a drink.

A woman came up to them. She was wearing a brightly colored skirt, banded with blue and red cloth, a low-cut yellow blouse, large, dangling earrings made of silver and turquoise. She carried a small wooden tray.

"What'll you gentleman have?" she asked. "You'll never make it to the bar."

"Whiskeys," Jeff said before Lew could say anything.

"Give me two dollars," she said.

Jeff whistled, but gave her two dollars. She disappeared, melting through the crowd that parted to let her pass.

"I hope she brings us something to drink," Jeff said. "Anyone with a tray could do that. Just take our money and go out the back door."

"You're mighty suspicious, Jeff."

155

"I'm skeptical of most everything in a city like this. This is the kind of town our preacher used to preach against when I was a kid. A regular Sodom."

"Or a Gomorrah."

"I don't see Wayne nowheres," Jeff said.

"I wouldn't know him if I saw him."

The woman did not return. Instead, a burly man who looked like a bouncer approached them. He handed Jeff back the two dollars.

"Leave," he said to Jeff.

"Why?"

"Sheriff Smith don't want you in here."

Jeff took the two dollars. The man glared at them, his hands on his hips as if ready to do battle.

Jeff put the money in his pocket and turned to leave.

A man leaned over to Lew and whispered, "Watch yourself."

Lew looked at him. "Why?"

"Outside. They'll be waiting for you."

The burly man came up and started shoving Jeff toward the door.

In moments, they were outside, the noise of the cantina muffled as the door slammed behind them.

"Let's get out of here," Lew said.

They had taken two steps when Lew saw

something flash from the shadows. The light from one of the cantina windows caught it, just for an instant.

Lew grabbed Jeff and pulled him down as he went into a crouch, clawing for his gun.

A pistol exploded, filling the dark with an orange flame.

An instant later, there was no longer time for Lew to think.

15

Jeff grunted and Lew knew he had been hit. He shoved his friend to the ground and cleared leather, hammering back on the Colt. He fired at the afterimage of the orange flame, then dove for the dirt. Two more pistols opened up and Lew rolled away toward the opposite side of the street. He fired once, then again.

Jeff moaned in pain.

Then Lew heard footsteps pounding as the gunmen ran away. The sounds faded and it was quiet. The people in the cantina probably hadn't heard a thing, he thought. He waited a few seconds, then crabbed over to where Jeff lay. He reached down and felt something sticky on his hand. He had touched Jeff's side.

"Who?" Jeff gasped in pain.

"I don't know. Jeff, you've been hit. I'm going to carry you out of here. Try and hold on."

Jeff did hold on until Lew got him to the hotel. He told the night clerk to send a doctor up to the room.

"It'll cost you," the clerk said.

"I'll pay. Just get us a doctor, right away."

"Right away, sir."

Lew laid Jeff out on the bed in Jeff's room. He found the lamp on the dresser and groped for a box of matches that he knew was there. Jeff's room was just like his. He struck a match, lifted the chimney, and lighted the wick. He adjusted the flame and slid the glass chimney back in place. He carried the lamp over to the nightstand next to the bed and set it down. Then he walked back to the dresser.

He poured water from the pitcher on the highboy into a bowl and soaked a small towel in it. He ripped Jeff's shirt and washed the blood away. Some was still pumping out around a small black hole rimmed with pale blue flesh.

"Lew," Jeff rasped, "in my boot. Cash. For Carol."

"You just hold on, Jeff. The doc's on his way. He'll fix you up in no time."

Jeff raised his hand, beckoned to Lew.

Lew leaned over to hear what Jeff had to say in his halting speech.

"I won't," Jeff said. "Make it. Drowning.

159

Hard to breathe. Take my. Boots off. Money for Carol."

Jeff's breathing was labored, shallow. His lips had turned bluish. Lew could see that his friend was in a bad way. He picked up the towel and wiped Jeff's forehead. Sweat had beaded up in the deep furrows. His face was pale, turning waxen in the lamplight.

Lew didn't take Jeff's boots just then. Instead, he stuffed a small piece of towel into the bullet hole to stanch the flow of blood. Jeff passed out as a shudder of pain rippled through his body. A few minutes later, Lew heard a knock. Not on Jeff's door, but on his own. He went to the door, opened it, saw a man with a black satchel standing in front of his door.

"Lew Zane?"

"Yeah, but it's Jeff Stevens who's hurt. In here."

"I'm Doc Renfrew," he said as he entered Jeff's room. He walked over to the bed, set his satchel on one end of it, and opened it. He took out a stethoscope and put it around his neck.

"Would have been here quicker," Renfrew said, "but Charlie, the clerk here, said you had been shot. I wanted to get some pine tar in case I needed it."

Renfrew was efficient. He put the cup of

the stethoscope on Jeff's chest, lifted one hand, and touched the wrist with two fingers.

"Heartbeat could be better. It's skipping a beat, a couple of beats every so often. His pulse is thready, too. Shock."

"I put a towel in the wound to stop the bleeding," Lew said.

"I see that. Not the best way to stop the bleeding, but it probably helped. Did he lose a lot of blood?"

"I don't know," Lew said.

Renfrew pulled the towel out of the wound and turned Jeff over on his side for a better look. "Hmm," he said.

"What's 'Hmm' mean?"

"It means it's a clean hole and the bullet's probably still inside. I'll check."

He turned Jeff over, rolling him from side to side so that he could see if the bullet had come out or was still inside.

"What's your friend's name again? I always like to know the name of my patients."

"Jeff Stevens."

"Stevens. Sounds familiar."

"It's a common enough name."

"To be sure. Well, I'm going in after the bullet. Here, take this."

The doctor reached into his bag and

pulled out a flat stick that seemed to have been planed down from a cut stick of lumber.

"What's this for?" Lew asked.

"If he wakes up, you poke that stick between his teeth and hold him down by the shoulders. I'm going to take his shirt off and then probe for the bullet."

"What are his chances, Doc?"

"Ah, the question."

"The question?"

"The most asked question, I should have said. People want to know how long they have to live, but when someone's hurt badly, the question is 'What are his or her chances?' "

"And the answer?"

"I don't know. Only God does."

"I understand," Lew said, turning the stick over and over in his hand.

Doc Renfrew cut away Jeff's shirt, tossed it onto the floor. Then he pulled out a long metal probe with a little hook at the end. To Lew, it looked like a heavy piece of wire that had been bent to make the hook. But whoever had done it had used a vise, most probably, because the piece of metal was straight and uniform.

"Bring me that bowl over on the dresser, will you, Mr. Zane?"

Lew took the bowl to the doctor. Renfrew set it down on the floor, held the probe over it, and poured alcohol over it.

"To sterilize it," he said. "I brought some whiskey if he wakes up."

"You a surgeon?" Lew asked.

"I am. Served in the Army, was with Zeb Pike when he came out this way. I loved the country, came back to stay. Now, let me get at this little booger."

The doctor knelt down beside the bed, moved the lamp to throw light on the wound, and then stuck the probe in very slowly and carefully. He looked up as he went deeper, as if listening for a sound. Deeper and deeper he went, then stopped.

"Find it?" Lew asked.

"I think so. Just below the liver, though it might have nicked it. I think it's buried in his large intestine, but could be in his abdomen. I'll know in a minute. Ah, here we go."

The doctor moved the probe up and down and twisted it around. He pulled a little bit, then moved the probe. Then he pulled again.

"It's inching its way out. Won't take long."

Jeff stirred, but did not wake up.

"Hold him down, Mr. Zane, just in case."

Lew stuck the piece of wood in his back pocket, went to the head of the bed, and placed his hands on Jeff's shoulders.

Renfrew continued to work the bullet toward the entry wound with deft and delicate manipulation of the probe. Jeff began to squirm. Lew put pressure on his shoulders.

"Just a little bit more," the doctor said.

Beads of sweat broke out once again on Jeff's brow and he made a low moaning sound in his throat.

The doctor stopped pulling on the probe. He set it down on the bed and reached into the wound, pried the flesh apart slightly, and grasped the lead bullet with his thumb and forefinger. He pulled it out and held it up to the light.

"There we are," Renfrew said.

Lew felt a little sick to his stomach as he stared at the bloody slug.

"A nice addition to my collection," Renfrew said, then pulled a thong out of his shirt. There, in a string, were other bullets, neatly drilled, dangling from a necklace.

"Those are all bullets?" Lew said.

"Ah, not just bullets, Mr. Zane. These are bullets I've removed from wounds since I came to Pueblo. As you can see, this is a violent town. A lot of shootings."

"Did . . . I mean, are those bullets from people who are walking around now? Alive?"

Renfrew shook his head and got to his feet.

"No, alas, some of the victims died. But not from lead poisoning."

The doctor pocketed the bullet after wiping it on the damp towel, and then reached into his bag. He brought out a small jar of unguent. He opened the jar and then picked up the probe again. He wrapped the probe with cotton, which he wound around it until it was tightly packed. Then he smeared the unguent on the cotton. The soft material had a pungent odor.

"Pine tar and gunpowder," Renfrew said. "My own concoction. I wish I had a hot poker, but I don't."

He then gently pushed the probe inside Jeff's wound and twirled it around. He did this four more times, then covered the tip of his finger with the unguent and pushed it into the wound, leaving some on the outside.

"Now, then," Renfrew said, and reached into his pocket for a box of matches. He lit one and touched it to the unguent. It caught fire. The flames raced along the pepperings of gunpowder, clear into the wound.

Jeff jumped and cried out in pain.

Lew jammed the stick between his teeth as the fire burned, cauterizing the wound.

Renfrew stepped away and looked down at Jeff.

"That'll stop the bleeding, help him to heal more quickly."

"Then Jeff will be all right?" Lew said, pressing down hard on Jeff's shoulders as the wounded man writhed and kicked, tried to scream.

"I don't know. He could develop peritonitis and die. Depends on what the bullet ripped when it went in there. The liver will heal if it's been cut. The intestine might cauterize over any tears in it. Hard to tell. I'll give you some powders, some morphine for the pain. You'll just have to watch him and see. If you see any sign of him failing, just send for me and I'll see what I can do."

"How far away are you?"

"Oh, I live in the hotel. My office is a few doors down. The clerk will know where I am."

The ignited gunpowder died out and Jeff stopped struggling.

"The pine tar will seal it pretty well," Renfrew said. He then began to wrap a bandage around Jeff's waist. "Watch this bandage and if there's any more blood, send for me. He might leak a little, but I think we burned all the little blood vessels pretty nicely."

Lew felt his stomach turn again when he

thought about what he had just witnessed.

"I'll keep an eye on him, Doc."

"Where did this shooting take place, by the way?" Renfrew asked.

"We were in the Double Eagle. A man kicked us out. Someone was waiting for us. The first shot hit Jeff and he went down."

"The Double Eagle, you say. Bad place that."

"It was crowded. We could hardly move in there."

"You came in between fights."

"Huh?"

"They have cockfights out back. In between, the patrons all come in, get more drinks, then go back outside to bet on the fighting cocks."

"I wondered. Seemed like an awful lot of people jammed in there."

"There's another thing, Mr. Zane. You probably didn't look up, but there's another story to that establishment. When you came in, someone was watching you from a slit-hole up there at the far end of the room."

"I didn't notice."

"Well, if they wouldn't sell you a drink, they wanted you outside so they could kill or rob you. You had a very close call, if you ask me."

"You've run into this before?" Lew asked.

"Sadly, yes. I've complained to the authorities, the sheriff, the judge, but to no avail. Too many shootings happen at that place. Someone wanted you dead, Mr. Zane. You or your friend Jeff here."

Lew eased up on Jeff, who had stopped struggling. He removed the stick from Jeff's mouth. Jeff's eyes fluttered, but he remained still. Then he opened his mouth.

"Wayne," Jeff breathed, and the doctor looked startled.

Lew stared down at Jeff, wondering if he knew for sure who had shot him.

Renfrew stiffened and his eyes clouded over as if they were filled with smoke.

For a long time there was only the sound of the flame sputtering as the wick in the lamp burned low.

16

Renfrew appeared startled when Lew looked at him, as if some bolt of recognition had struck him like lightning.

He walked over to the head of the bed and looked at Jeff. He leaned down to speak to him.

"Did you say Wayne?" he asked Jeff.

"Wayne done it. Shot me."

"Wayne Smith?"

"Yeah."

Renfrew stood up, looked at Lew again.

"Now I know where I heard that name before. I treated two children several months ago. They both had earaches and a woman brought them in. Her name was Carol Smith. But as I was examining her children, a boy and a girl, she said her maiden name was Stevens. She even mentioned that her father's name was Jeffrey. Is this the same man?"

"Yes, Doc. Jeff Stevens is Carol's father.

He rode out from Missouri to see her."

"Good Lord. What a small world. And Wayne Smith is a deputy sheriff here in town. With a bad reputation, I'm afraid."

"Yeah, we know. I don't think Jeff knows who shot him. He just thinks it was his son-in-law."

"I've treated a number of patients who were hurt at the Double Eagle. Only one or two were shot, however. Most were beaten. And robbed. Why would Wayne Smith want to kill his father-in-law?"

"I don't know, Doc. Guilty conscience maybe."

"That man has no conscience. I do know he took his wife and kids up to Leadville, then returned by himself. I never knew why. I never asked him and he never told me."

"You know Smith?"

"He's brought in a prisoner or two who needed medical attention. I gathered this was distasteful to him, but he was following orders from the sheriff himself, Andrew Coolidge. Andy means well, but he's tied to politics tighter than a tick to a dog's behind. I asked Andy once why he hired such a man as Smith, and he just shrugged and said that Wayne kept the drunks off the street in broad daylight."

"A hell of a reason to hire a man like

170

Smith," Lew said.

"Well, you and Jeff here had no business going to the Double Eagle. Smith lives there at night when he's off duty, and I've heard stories about a woman named Flora who works there. She looks out that peephole up in the second story and picks out who she's going to rob. Did you by chance pay money for drinks and a man gave your money back to you?"

"That's exactly what happened."

"The man who gave you your money back and who told you to leave was probably Ed McDermott. He's a tough who beats people up there when they get loud or rowdy. I've had to sew a lot of stitches in the heads of men he's thrown out of the Double Eagle, and wire up a jaw or two he's broken. You'd be wise to give the Double Eagle a wide berth, Mr. Zane."

Lew said nothing. He watched as the doctor packed up his instruments, put away his stethoscope. He laid some packets of powders on the nightstand and closed his bag.

"That will be four dollars, Mr. Zane, and I thank you."

Lew paid him, counting out four one-dollar bills.

"I'm in Room 200, if you need me. Sleep is what Mr. Stevens needs right now. Let the wound calm down, the blood coagulate. The packets are clearly labeled. Give him the morphine only as a last resort."

Lew let the doctor out, then sat at the small table in the center of the room.

He looked over at Jeff, who seemed to be sleeping soundly and peacefully. His face was flushed, but he was breathing normally, even and deep. After a while, Lew turned up the wick on the lamp. He sat in the easy chair, stretched out his legs, and closed his eyes. He would not enjoy the luxury of sleeping in a bed that night, he knew. And he hoped he would not have to take Jeff's boots off, except to make him more comfortable. The idea that Jeff might die made his blood run hot with anger.

There was no reason for Wayne Smith to kill Jeff. Or if there was, Lew didn't know what that reason might be. Could it be that Jeff had not told him all of the story about Wayne and Carol? And himself? Had there been trouble between Jeff and his son-in-law back in Missouri, trouble that Jeff had never mentioned?

Lew did not know. But for a man to kill another, he ought to have a damned good reason. He wondered what Wayne's reason was.

After a fitful night of dozing and sleeping

in the chair, Lew awoke with a stiff neck and numb feet. His mouth was dry and the lamp had burned out. Dawn light seeped through the shades over the windows. Jeff was a dark hulk on the bed, still lying on his back, his breathing labored.

Lew walked over to the window and pulled up the shade. Light sprayed across part of the bed, enough for Lew to take a look at Jeff.

Jeff's face was pale, the redness all gone, as if the blood had drained out of it overnight.

As he looked at Jeff more closely, Lew saw a small trickle of froth spittle at the corner of Jeff's mouth. He felt the bandage. It was dry, but as he bent down to examine it, he detected a strong odor, and the odor was foul.

Lew picked up the towel and wiped the corner of Jeff's mouth. He touched his lips. They were dry. He got a glass and poured water in it, set it on the nightstand in case Jeff woke up and was thirsty. Then he stretched and ran his fingers over the faint stubble on his own chin.

Jeff moaned and then his eyes opened, closed again.

"Too bright for you, Jeff?" Lew said.

"No. I heard water splash. Can you give

me a drink of water?"

"Sure."

Lew propped Jeff up, held the glass of water to his lips. He tipped it and Jeff began to drink. He choked on the first swallow, then as his tissues lost their dryness, he was able to drink half the water in the glass. He gasped when he was finished and looked down at his waist.

"Trussed up, eh?"

"The doc got the bullet out, Jeff."

"I don't remember."

"That's all right. Do you remember getting shot?"

"Barely."

"You said last night that Wayne shot you. Did you see him?"

"No, but it was Wayne Smith all right. That bastard."

"Why would he shoot you?"

"Ahhhh," Jeff said, and leaned back on the pillow.

"You know, don't you?"

Jeff nodded.

"Were you going there to kill Wayne last night? Is that why he shot you?"

Jeff shook his head. "I went there to see if Wayne knew."

"If he knew what?"

"Before Wayne took Carol away, there was

a scandal in Bolivar. A large amount of money was found missing from the town treasury. No one knew who had taken it. But I saw Wayne hide a keg in the shed in back of my house. I looked inside the keg and found the money. I didn't tell anyone until Carol told me that Wayne was taking her away. I told her about the keg, saying that she was leaving with a thief. She didn't believe me until she got to Pueblo and found a keg among their belongings. It was full of stolen money. She wrote me and told me to expose Wayne as the thief. I said that I would, and that I would be a witness against him."

"So Carol must have shown Wayne that letter. Or else he read it without her knowing."

"She showed it to him. She wrote that he went into a rage and said he'd kill me if I ever told anyone that he had taken the money."

"Now I understand."

"I wrote Carol that it was too late. I had told the mayor and the chief of police and they had sworn out a warrant for Wayne's arrest. I didn't tell her that I had signed an affidavit about the stolen money in case anything ever happened to me."

"So Wayne thinks you'll testify against him

if he's brought back to Bolivar?"

"He knows I will, yes. But that's not the worst part. Wayne is wanted for murder."

"Murder?" Lew said.

"He took the money from a clerk who was auditing the city's finances. He cut his throat and took the money. I found the bloody knife in the same shed where Wayne hid the money, and I gave it to the sheriff. He showed it to the owner of the hardware store, who remembered selling the knife to Wayne, and not only that, but Wayne had carved his initials in the bone handle of the knife. Plain as day."

"But Wayne got away with it. He'll never go back to Bolivar on his own."

"Before I left, the mayor got a judge to issue a fugitive warrant for Wayne's arrest. The federal government is looking for him now."

"You played a dangerous game last night, Jeff. If Wayne killed for that money, he wouldn't even blink to kill you."

"I wanted to tell him that there's a federal warrant out for his arrest. It was dumb of me, I know."

"Dumb and dangerous. You're probably not safe here, even."

"Well, if you'll get my pistol and put it here by my side, I'll shoot Wayne if he walks through that door."

Lew tried not to laugh. But he snickered at the idea that Jeff could get the drop on a wary man like Wayne Smith.

"I'll watch over you while you heal up," Lew said. "You don't need a pistol in your condition."

"I do feel pretty weak."

The talking had worn Jeff out. His pallor was waxen, and he was sweating again. He drank more water, then closed his eyes.

Lew paced the room. He was hungry, and yet he didn't know if he dared leave Jeff alone while he went out for something to eat. Jeff would be hungry, too, he thought.

"Jeff," Lew said as he stood over the wounded man, "I'm going out to get us some vittles. I'll lock the door when I leave. If anyone knocks, you don't say a word. Hear?"

"I hear, Lew. I won't say nothing."

"Just sit tight."

Jeff tried to laugh, but he winced in pain with the effort. He opened his eyes and closed them again. His breathing did not sound good to Lew.

Lew left, locking the door to Jeff's room behind him. He walked to the front desk and asked where he could get some food to take up to his room.

"There's a little Mexican café one block over that's open early. They can give you a basket. You leave a deposit and they return your money when you bring the basket back. It's called Lupe's. Nice lady who runs it."

"Don't let anyone in our rooms," Lew said.

"No, sir. Of course not."

"I mean nobody."

The clerk's face turned ashen. He was a young, nervous fellow anyway, and his hands began to tremble as he stood at the counter.

"No, sir, I won't," he said. "But I get off in a few minutes. John Bascomb is on the day shift. He's my older brother. I'm Charlie Bascomb."

"Charlie, you tell your brother what I told you."

"Yes, sir, I will."

Lew left, walking with rapid steps down the deserted street. The sun was up, streaming through the streets, lighting up the sides of buildings, making shadows in between them. He hoped he was doing the right thing, leaving Jeff alone like that. His worry was probably needless, but Wayne sounded like a desperate man to him. A man who would stop at nothing to protect himself and his ill-gotten gains.

And as Lew looked at the few people he passed, the bad thing was that he had no idea what Wayne Smith looked like. Would he be wearing a badge on his vest or did he keep it in his pocket? Was he tall, short, fat, skinny?

When he got back to the hotel, Lew promised himself he'd ask Jeff for a description of Wayne Smith.

As he turned the corner to go down to the next street, Lew felt a shadow fall over him. He started to turn, but it was too late. He saw an arm, part of a face, and then felt a crushing blow to his skull. Lights danced in his head, and then he felt himself falling, falling into blackness.

Then, everything turned dark and his mind went blank.

17

Someone splashed water in Lew's face. He awoke, spluttering, his head spinning, filled with cotton. He was dizzy, and it took him a few seconds to realize he was lying flat on his back, with people standing around, looking down at him. The fog in his brain lifted slowly, and he became aware of the pain in the back of his head. It felt as if an anvil had been dropped on it. He sat up and touched the sore spot. There was a knot there, and a small cut in the knot. Whoever had struck him had hit him very hard.

"Mister, you ought not to drink so much," a man said. "Not in this town. Looks like you got rolled."

Lew fixed his eyes on the man who had spoken. His face swam there like a balloon with eyes and hair and mouth, bobbing in and out of the fog, weaving as if it were on a tether.

"Not drunk," Lew said, his voice sounding far away, lost in the ringing of his ears.

He looked down, saw that his pockets were turned inside out. He patted the gun in his holster, felt a sense of relief. But the keys to his and Jeff's rooms were gone. He struggled to his feet, first pulling himself to his knees, then, extending both arms, pushing up until he broke free of the ground and was standing on two feet. His legs felt wobbly and it took him a few seconds to clear his head. He leaned against the wall of the building, one arm extended for support.

"We just saw you a-lyin' here, stranger," another man said. "Figured you was drunk. Sorry. Say, you got a nasty bump on your head."

"Somebody knocked me out," Lew said. "Did you see what happened? Any of you?"

There were two men and a woman standing there. They all shook their heads.

"Nope," the first man said. "We were just walking along and seen you lyin' stretched out. Common sight here in Pueblo."

"Thanks. I'll be all right."

Lew lurched away from the three people and headed back to the hotel. A sense of dread came over him as he thought about those missing keys.

Charlie was not at the front desk. Nobody was.

Lew took the stairs two at a time, rushed to Jeff's hotel door. It was slightly ajar. He entered and saw two men standing by Jeff's bed. He could not see Jeff. One of the men was standing at the foot of the bed, blocking Lew's view.

"Doctor," Lew said, recognizing the other man.

"Oh, there you are. I wondered where you were. Bad news, I'm afraid."

Lew's heart plummeted in his chest.

"Your friend, Mr. Stevens, is gone."

The man at the foot of the bed turned, and Lew saw the resemblance.

"You Charlie's brother?" Lew said.

"Yes. Are you Mr. Zane?"

"I am."

"Charlie said I was not to let anyone upstairs to this room, but the man who came up acted as if he had a room here, or was here on business. Besides, I knew him. I mean, I knew who he was. He was a deputy sheriff."

"Let me guess. Wayne Smith." Lew felt the bottom go out of his stomach as if the floor had given way and he had fallen two stories.

"Why, yes. Deputy Smith came down a few minutes later. I asked him if everything was all right and he said yes, that it was."

"Bascomb," Lew said, "you're not only stupid, you're dumber than a sack full of dead possums. Smith probably murdered that man on the bed there."

Bascomb's face drained to a washed-out roan color.

"Doc, what happened to Jeff?"

"Well, I'm just now looking, Mr. Zane. He's dead. Been dead a half hour or so. There's a bruise on his neck. I'm feeling for a possible fracture of the hyoid bone now."

"What's that?" Lew asked.

"If it's broken, it could mean that Mr. Stevens was strangled to death."

Lew stepped in close.

Jeff's eyes were shut, his mouth open. He wasn't breathing. Lew felt his stomach muscles tauten. Bands tightened around his chest, as if he were being smothered. The doctor was feeling Jeff's neck with two fingers.

"Yep. This man was strangled."

"What brought you to Jeff's room?" Lew asked.

"I was going to my office, thought I'd stop in and see how Jeff was doing. The door was open and I just walked in. When I saw that Jeff was dead, I summoned John here to witness the death certificate after I determined the cause of death."

"So have you done that?"

"I'm going to rule this a homicide. Jeff was clearly strangled to death."

"Will there be an investigation?" Lew asked.

"There'll be a coroner's inquest, yes."

"What's that?"

"The coroner will examine the body, verify a cause of death. If he determines that my diagnosis is correct, he'll hold a hearing to determine who might have murdered Mr. Stevens."

"And then?" Lew asked.

"The coroner will call witnesses, including John Bascomb here, possibly Sheriff Smith, and then a jury will decide who's to be charged with Mr. Stevens's murder, if anyone."

"That's how it works, huh?"

"That's how it works in Pueblo," the doctor said.

"And if Wayne Smith is charged with Jeff's murder, then what?"

"The prosecuting attorney will swear out a warrant for his arrest before a judge. The judge will call a jury and Smith will go on trial."

"It happens that way every time, right?"

"Well, it's supposed to happen that way. Whether or not it does in this case, I couldn't say."

Lew could feel his anger rising. None of this had happened with Fritz Canby and Wiley Pope. The judge had just looked the other way. Those boys had gone scot-free and they had killed the only witness against them. There had been no justice in that case, and he didn't think he could expect any in this case, either. He looked at Bascomb, who stood there running a finger under his tight collar as if to loosen it so he could breathe better.

"What about you, Bascomb? Will you testify that you saw Smith come up to this room?"

"Well, I actually didn't see where Sheriff Smith went when he came upstairs. He could have gone to any of the rooms."

"But you know where he went, don't you?"

"Not at all. I can't testify to what I didn't see, Mr. Zane."

"No, I suppose not. The ostrich can't see when it buries its head in the sand, either, can it?"

"I don't know," Bascomb said.

"Mr. Zane," Doc Renfrew said, "I'll arrange to have the body taken to the coroner's office. He's the local funeral director.

Let me take a look at that bump on your head."

"Fine," Lew said as the doctor examined his wound, "I'll pay all expenses for Jeff's burial."

"I'll tell Dean that."

"Dean?"

"Dean Vollmer. He's the undertaker and the coroner. You've got a bad bruise but you'll be okay."

"I'll be at the front desk if you need me, Mr. Zane. I'm sorry for your friend's death. The hotel assumes no liability whatsoever, of course. You understand that. We have no control over the behavior of our guests or their visitors."

"Yeah, I understand it, Bascomb. The ostrich."

Bascomb coughed and started for the door. The doctor put his stethoscope back in the bag and closed it. He started to leave, too, but he stopped and put a hand on Lew's shoulder.

"I'm sorry, Mr. Zane. I hope it works out for you and Mr. Stevens. If it's any comfort, I don't think he would have lived out the week, though."

"Oh? What makes you say that, Doc?"

"I think that bullet tore through his large intestine. Without an operation, I think he would have developed an infection and died. He might have died anyway. His age, the severity of the wound."

"You didn't say that last night."

"I'm always hopeful."

"Yeah. Me, too. You know, it doesn't make any difference now how Jeff died. One man killed him, either way. Wayne Smith."

"I can't speculate on such matters, Mr. Zane."

Lew watched them go and then sat down on the bed. He and Jeff had come a long way together. They had gotten to be friends. Now, Jeff was dead. His daughter would never see him again.

He reached down and pulled off Jeff's boots. In one of them, there was an oilcloth filled with money. He counted out the bills. There was a total of 245 dollars. At the bottom of the bills, there was a folded piece of paper.

Lew opened it and read it.

"Dear Carol: If you get this money from Lew Zane, then you will know I am dead. Lew is my friend. I told him to give you the money. I leave you all my worldly goods. You take good care of those kids. Your loving old dad."

Lew sighed. Now, he was truly obligated to find Carol Smith and give her the money her father had left her. It was an obligation and a duty he could not deny. He wrapped the packet back up, along with the note, and slipped it into his pocket.

"I'll see to it that Carol gets this, Jeff," he said, feeling a little foolish speaking to a dead man.

But then, maybe his words hadn't sounded that foolish. Maybe Jeff could hear him, wherever he was. Maybe he was looking down on him in some other form.

"I'll get the bastard who killed you, too," Lew said, and since this was said mostly to himself, he did not feel foolish in saying it. He looked down at the floor and saw something that looked familiar. He reached down and picked it up, knowing then what it was. His room key. Jeff's was probably still in the door.

Wayne must have followed him out of the hotel and seen his chance to do away with Jeff. Wayne waited, probably knowing where he was headed, then struck him over the head, taken the keys, come back to the hotel, and strangled Jeff. But could Lew prove it? And if he did prove it, did that guarantee that justice would be done?

He put Jeff's boots back on and left the room to go to his own. He closed Jeff's door behind him, saw the key in it, locked the door, and put the key in his pocket. He would give it only to the coroner when he came for Jeff's body.

Later that afternoon, after Jeff's body had been removed from the hotel, Lew walked over to the Double Eagle. It was open, but quiet. He walked in, saw a lone bartender behind the bar. A few patrons sat at tables, some playing cards, others smoking and talking. He ordered a whiskey and then looked up, saw the black boards on the second story. There were long slits cut out of them that he could barely see.

"Mind if I walk out back?"

"Sure," the bartender said, "go ahead. Cockfights start at eight tonight."

Lew walked through the back door and out to a large courtyard. There was a wire strung across the sandy arena, bleacher seats on three sides. There was a sign on a board hanging from the wire. The sign said FA-VORITO. The word meant nothing to Jeff, but he saw that the sign would slide from one side of the arena to the other, if pushed.

The arena had been cleaned up, raked, the blood from the roosters removed. The arena looked ready for business that night.

Back inside, Lew finished his whiskey, took his change from the bar.

"Another?" The bartender was young,

with a face that hadn't been shaved much.

"No, thanks. I may come back tonight."

"Good luck at the cockfights."

Lew left the saloon and walked back to the hotel. He should leave, he thought. Let the law take care of Wayne Smith. It was none of his business. He should ride on to Leadville and try to find Carol Smith, give her the money.

That's what he should do, he knew.

But he couldn't get Wayne Smith out of his craw.

He felt the knot on the back of his head. The swelling had gone down, but it was still tender, sore.

A reminder, he thought, that he was dealing with a dangerous man.

18

After paying the undertaker for Jeff's burial and talking to the man, Lew made his decision.

"It will probably take me a month or so to hold an inquest," Dean Vollmer said when Lew counted out the money. "Then, depending on how busy the prosecutor is, and the courts, it could take up to half a year or more to arrest and prosecute someone for any crime that is revealed at the inquest."

"Justice moves slow in Pueblo," Lew said.

"We call it being careful. Evidence must be gathered, witnesses interviewed. It all takes time."

"I'll try and be back in town within a month," Lew said. "I want to testify at the inquest."

"It's just like a court. You have to tell the truth. Unless you were an eyewitness to a murder, you might not be called to testify."

"But I can watch, can't I?"

"An inquest is a public hearing. You can watch."

Lew saddled up Jeff's horse and his own. He got a map showing the way to Leadville. He stocked up on provisions he thought he'd need, and bought a heavy coat after learning that the weather could change fast in the mountains. One minute it could be warm, the next, freezing cold. He set out for Salida after settling his bill at the hotel. He made sure no one was following him as he led Jeff's horse and set out early. All four saddlebags were full. He had plenty of coffee, hardtack, beef jerky, and staples like flour, beans, salt, and sugar.

When he rode into the mountains, the world changed. Autumn was already there in all its splendor. The aspen leaves shone golden in the sun, the air was crisp and sharp, and the blue sky was flocked with puffy white clouds. He passed many wagons heading down to Pueblo, many of these loaded with ore from the lead and silver mines. Some of the men he encountered told him it was their last trip. They would not return until after the spring thaw.

He did not linger long in Salida. He saw the rough cob of a town with its wagons and carts jamming the streets, its bearded, rugged men with small eyes and big noses, clothing saturated with dust and grime, its pinch-faced women with their gaudy skirts and hennaed hair, their rouged cheeks and lampblack eyelashes, and wondered at the odd mixture of humanity in such a small place. He had a hot meal at a small, crowded café called Betsy's Eats. The soup was greasy and the meat tough, but the coffee was strong and he rode out toward Leadville with a full, though sour, stomach.

The country grew wilder after Lew left Salida. The road got steeper in places, and his heart quickened when he saw mule deer, elk, and on the high slopes above timberline, the surefooted Rocky Mountain sheep with their formidable and majestic curved horns, standing regally in the sun looking down at him from above. He saw a few wagons just outside of Salida, but then he rode for miles without seeing a soul.

Until he heard the shot. He reined Ruben to a halt and listened as the sound reverberated through the canyons, echoed from the rimrock and the high bluffs until it was swallowed into silence. He pulled his rifle from its scabbard and jacked a cartridge into the chamber. He ticked Ruben's flanks with both spurs and moved out, the reins of Jeff's horse looped and knotted through a D-ring on his saddle.

He rounded a bend in the trail, and through the trees ahead, saw a wide meadow. A man stood over a horse, cursing until the air was smoking with his frosty breath.

"Damn you, Baldy, you dumb sonofabitch. You bow-legged, cross-eyed, miserable blue-balled bastard."

Lew approached slowly, rifle at the ready, butt resting on his leg, his finger inside the trigger guard behind the trigger. He could twirl it in a moment, shift his finger in front of the trigger, and shoot from the hip in a twinkling if need be.

The man spotted Lew and turned away from the horse, smoke still curling out of the barrel of his pistol.

"You there," the man called. "I'll give you two hundred dollars for that horse you're leading."

As Lew hesitated, the man holstered his pistol and started walking toward him.

"Damned fool horse," he said, "went and broke his dad-blamed leg in a damned hole. Had to shoot him dead, damn the dad-blamed luck. Way in hell out here in the middle of nowhere."

"Hold on," Lew said. "Where you headed?"

"Leadville. And I'll give you three hundred

dollars for that horse you ain't usin'. Got the money right here in my pocket. The name's Hardy, pilgrim, Jack Hardy."

The man stretched out his hand as he approached.

Lew didn't know what to make of him. He was a barrel-chested man, looked to be in his forties, with a round, grizzled face sprouting a five-inch beard, ears that stuck out like the handles on a jug of moonshine, no moustache, but a little pudgy mouth that gave him the look of a man who sucked on eggs. He had no neck that Lew could see, and his trousers were tucked into miner's boots that seemed not to have seen a shine since they left the store.

Lew leaned over, shook Hardy's hand.

"Where you headed?" Hardy said. "And I didn't catch your name."

"I'm Lew Zane. Going to Leadville."

"Why, that's just where I'm headed. If you'll sell me that horse."

"It's not mine to sell," Lew said.

"Well, maybe you'll let me rent it, then. I'll give you a hundred dollars just to ride that horse to Leadville."

Lew hesitated.

"Another hundred when we get there."

"I hate to take advantage of you, Hardy."

"Call me Jack. Hell, you're the first honest man I've seen up in these hills. I'll give you two hundred when we get to Leadville. Hell, there's more where this came from."

"That's a lot of money to rent a horse."

"Well, I got to get there. Time is money. I've got me a silver mine in Leadville, and I just come from the bank in Pueblo. Got to get one more mule train of ore out of the mine before winter sets in. It ain't that far, and I'm better company than you got now, just you and that extra horse."

"All right," Lew said. He slid his rifle back in its scabbard and loosened the knot in the D-ring, freeing the reins. He handed them to Hardy.

"Climb on, then. Horse's name is Leroy."

"You didn't steal it, did you?" Hardy said as he took the reins.

"No. It belongs to a friend of mine," Lew said.

"Where's your friend? Up in Leadville waiting for you?"

"He's dead."

"Jeez-amighty. What you doing with a dead man's horse?"

"Taking it up to his daughter. Look, Hardy, anything you want off your horse? Saddle, saddlebags, bridle, blanket?"

"No. I'll have the boys stop by on the way down and pick up what's there, if nobody steals it. Hate to lose that good Santa Fe saddle, though. But I sure as hell don't want to tote it all the way up to Leadville."

"All right," Lew said. "Let's go. You lead out, seeing as you know the way."

"Here's a hundred dollars, Lew. On account."

Hardy cackled as he handed over the money in crisp new bills.

Lew took the bills, stuffed them in his trouser pocket.

"Just don't shoot me in the back, Lew. You wouldn't do that, would you?"

"Not unless I had good reason," Lew said. "And money wouldn't be one."

"Hey, you'd do to ride the river with. A regular Good Samaritan you are."

"I'd hate to be afoot in this country."

"The horse feels good under me," Hardy said. "Missouri trotter, eh?"

"Yep. Just don't break his leg. I might have to shoot you both."

Hardy laughed. "You got a sense of humor, I see. Makes me feel a mite better about riding in front of you."

But they rode side by side. Hardy was a talker and he enjoyed talking about himself and his lucky strike in Leadville the year before. He told Lew that his wagons would be back up in a few days, having hauled a lot of ore down to the smelters in Pueblo.

"After the big gold strikes in '59 and '60, the gold played out and the miners left, leaving big old holes in the mountains. Then some fellers from another state come into Leadville and looked at the tailings and such."

"What are tailings?"

"The rock they dug out of the mines and didn't smelt. Anyways, it wasn't only tailings these fellers looked at. The miners who were using placers, rockers, pans, kept complaining about all the black stuff that was so hard to get off the gold. Made them work harder than they wanted to. But that black stuff, as we found out last year, was silver."

"Silver?"

"That's right. These two fellers started buying up all the old gold mines that were played out. I got me a grubstake and along with old Haw Tabor and others, we started mining silver. I bought a claim for fifty dollars, I tell you, and I've made a fortune. Tabor's richer than Croesus, and so are a lot of other men. That why you're going up to Leadville? Most all of the mines is bought up."

"No, but I'm looking for a job."

"You are? What kind of job?"

"I don't know. I hadn't thought about it that much, but I've got to eat. And I may be up here or in Pueblo for quite a while."

"What can you do?"

"I'm good with horses. I can milk a cow. I can do a little carpenter work."

Hardy laughed.

"Not much call for any of that up here in Leadville. Can't raise horses or cattle in the high country, 'cept in summer. No milking that I know of."

"I guess I'm a farmer," Lew said. "Don't know much else."

"You're packing iron and you look like you know what to do with that Winchester."

"Tools, Hardy, just tools."

"The way you wear that Colt, I'd reckon you've done more than pound nails with it."

Lew felt a tightening in his throat, heat flushing through the tiny veins beneath his face. Hardy was more observant than Lew would have liked.

"I believe in a man having the right to defend himself, Jack."

"And have you done some defending?"

"A little."

"Ah, that puts a different light on your quest for employment."

"It does? How so?"

"Maybe you want a job as a lawman."

Lew stiffened.

"No, sir. Not me."

"You sound as though you got a distaste for such a job. But there's men making a pretty good living at that trade."

Lew said nothing. He thought of Wayne Smith. If he was the caliber of men the law was looking for, Lew wanted no part of that profession. His memory of Billy Jim Colfax was still bitter in his mouth, as well.

"Tell you what, Lew," Hardy said. "After you deliver this horse to your friend's daughter, you look me up. I've got the Little Nellie Mine. I might could use you."

"To do what?"

"Let's just say you'd have to use those tools you carry."

"Legal or illegal?" Lew asked.

"Does it make any difference?"

"Yes, it sure does, Jack. I may not want to work as a lawman, but I don't want to be on the wrong side of the law either."

Hardy laughed. "Legal, then. Good pay. But . . ."

"But what?" Lew said.

"We'll talk about the 'but' when you come see me. Let's leave it at that. If you want a job, I think I can fix you up. I got to give it some thought, too."

"Fair enough," Lew said.

But he wondered what kind of job Hardy had in mind. He didn't intend to stay long in Leadville. He wanted to get back to Pueblo and attend that coroner's inquest. He wanted to see what kind of justice would prevail out West.

As they rode, Lew felt Hardy's eyes on him, as if he was sizing him up. He knew nothing about mining and Hardy knew that. What bothered him most was that the job might be one that involved gunplay, and if it was, Lew would turn him down.

He thought wryly: *A man who lives by the gun dies by the gun.*

He hoped Hardy wasn't barking up that tree.

19

Faron Briggs knew he had made a big mistake.

He should never have let the men in the wagon train chase after those marauding Cherokee. When they came back, two days later, they were missing two men, and those who did come back were wounded. And scared.

One man was hurt so badly with a broken leg, shattered by a Cherokee war club, that they couldn't move for over a week. Another had two lead balls in his hide, one in the rump, the other in his leg, and Faron had to pull them out and burn the wounds shut with a red-hot poker.

"Cal, I told you not to chase after them redskins. Now, look at you. And two good men gone, wasted on your wild-goose chase. Chasing after revenge."

"I know, I know. God, Faron, I hate what I done. I feel real bad." Calvin Morton lay in the wagon on his stomach, his wife, Betty, staring at his rump as if mesmerized, her eyes as fixed and vacant as the buttons on her dress. The smell of burning flesh filled the wagon, making her sick to her stomach.

"Didn't you hear that man Lew telling us not to chase after them Cherokee?"

"I — I heard him. God, Faron, I paid the price. Don't keep after me on it."

"You hush, Cal," Betty said, coming out of her stupor, turning her head to gulp in air. "You keep on, you'll start bleeding again."

Faron eased himself out of the wagon, a look of disgust on his face.

"Don't cover that up, Betty. Just let him lie there on his belly until that butt wound scabs over. We've got to keep movin'. We've already lost near two weeks of time with all this."

"I'll take care of Calvin, Faron," she said. "You do what you have to do."

The other wounds were not as serious. Jim Becker was walking stiff-legged. A Cherokee bullet had creased his left leg, just below the knee. It was more like a burn than a bullet wound. And Frank Eakins had lost a thumb, shot off when he was turning his horse to get away from his attackers. He had lost some blood and he was in pain, but he could still ride and shoot. Ned Willis had had an arrow glance off his forehead, shearing off a chunk of flesh, but he wouldn't die from it.

The wounded men all had sheepish looks on their faces when Faron gave the order to move out. All of them had rifles, and were nervous as their wives took up the reins and released the brakes.

"You figure they'll come at us again, Faron?" Willis asked as Faron rode to the head of the wagon train.

"You can damned sure bet on it, Ned. You boys got 'em real mad, I'm thinkin'."

"Aw, you go to hell, Briggs," Willis said, cracking the reins atop the backs of his mules.

Briggs rode ahead of the three wagons, gazing out at the prairie, scanning the tall grass for any sign of movement. Dissension among the pilgrims who had hired him had already made the trip to Santa Fe miserable, and the trouble with renegade Cherokee had added to his woes. Usually, he could pick men and women who had the grit and backbone to make such a trip without a great deal of bickering, but he had guessed wrong with these people. The men were all ornery, constantly complaining, whether it be over the heat, the long days, or the chilly nights. The women were a headstrong bunch and pushed their husbands mercilessly, nagging them day and night over small things, unnecessary things.

If the train wasn't moving fast enough for the women, they ragged their husbands to make the mules go faster. If the fire at night was too big or too small, they barked orders to their men like Army sergeants. Briggs had decided that the women were all fishwives, and the men a bunch of spineless whiners still tied to their wives' apron strings. They were about as useful as teats on a boar.

A covey of quail flushed in front of him with a brittle whir of wings, and Faron's heart jumped into a staccato beat. His horse stepped off course as if to run, but came back into line once he put pressure on the bit. A pair of doves hurtled past, their wings whistling, then vanished over the horizon. Faron cursed the slowness, the fact that they still had so far to go in dangerous country. Indians could hide in the tall grass and nobody would ever see them until it was too late.

He barely noticed the shallow gully, dry as a bone, when he rode through it, so lost was he in his thoughts. Had the gully been wet, he might have noticed, but he rode through it and climbed to the other side, back up to the flat. It was a lapse in judgment and observation he would come to regret. But his thoughts took him elsewhere, even though Faron knew better. A man who did not pay attention to the terrain, to the weather, to almost anything at all, sometimes came to a bad end.

At least they had left Oklahoma Territory behind and were in Kansas. Surely, the Cherokee would not stray so far from home, he thought. Indians were very careful about whose lands they crossed, or so he'd heard. Perhaps the danger was over and they would have no further encounters with hostile Indians. Not like in the old days, when such a crossing was fraught with peril and many a traveler's bones lay bleaching in the sun all along the Santa Fe Trail.

Faron daydreamed himself into aloneness. When he snapped out of his reverie and turned around to look back at the wagons, all he saw was an empty trail. He muttered under his breath and envisioned a broken wheel, a lame mule, or some such that must have halted the train.

"Ho, Willis," he called, and his voice seemed to fall back on him, swallowed up by the silence.

Faron turned his horse and started back to where the wagons should be. Then he stopped. He heard something, something that chilled his blood as if his veins had been filled with freezing water. A thud, then another. A crack that sounded like a bone breaking. A muffled cry, a stifled scream. More thudding sounds, and a squishing sound as if someone had smashed a melon with a ten-pound maul.

He rode back a few yards, and that's when he noticed a gap in the trail and realized that he had passed through a depression without realizing it. He halted a few yards from the rim of what he knew now was a gully and waited, listening. He heard something odd that took him several moments to decipher. The sound was like a series of whispers, or gasps, *whick, whick, whoop,* followed by *snick, snick,* then a slight jingling noise as if someone was jiggling a leather pouch full of brass rings. When he realized what it was, he slowly pulled his rifle from its boot, then slowly levered a round into its chamber. The sound of the metallic mechanism was drowned by louder sounds that he could easily identify, hoofbeats. Rapid hoofbeats that quickly faded away.

He eased his horse over the top rim of the gully and looked down into the center of it, some thirty or forty yards away. Faron could scarcely believe his eyes. The horror of what he saw froze his throat as if it were being clutched by an icy hand. He stared, not believing his eyes, and let his mind start putting pieces together, the sounds he had heard, the objects that now stood out in relief under the burning Kansas sun.

The cut traces lay scattered like flattened dead snakes in front of the wagons. Willis hung from the buckboard seat, a gaping red gash in his throat. His wife hung over the opposite side, her head dangling from a long grisly tendon, her hair obscuring her face.

Faron rode down into the gully, past the first wagon, dreading what he would see. There was an eerie silence that made his skin prickle on the back of his neck. More cut traces, the wagon tongue nothing more than a long skinned pole, angling into the ground. Next to the wagon, splayed on his back, lay Frank Eakins, the front of his skull caved in, his face drenched with blood, broken white teeth jutting out of the gelatinous mass. His privates had been cut off. There was a ragged tear in his trousers at the crotch. Then the last wagon, where Faron's stomach swirled with bile and his throat constricted as he fought to keep from vomiting.

Betty Morton lay slumped on the seat, the top of her head caved in as if from a single blow from a war club. Splinters of bone stuck out from under her cheekbones. Her face was squinched up so that she was barely recognizable. Her nose was no longer there; it had been mashed into her twisted mouth so that it resembled a mass of bloody dough.

Faron rode around to the back of the wagon, dreading what he would see. Cal Morton still had a hatchet buried in his chest. The breastbone had been split in two, his heart severed, leaving a tangle of arteries exposed like so many hollow worms. His throat was cut, as well, and it was plain to see the savagery of the attack.

The Cherokee had struck swiftly and silently.

None of those now dead had had the slightest chance to defend themselves. Faron could picture it in his mind as he looked up at the sides of the gully. The Indians must have been waiting on both sides, lying in the tall grass, waiting for the wagons to reach the bottom of the gully. They had sprung from their hiding places and leaped down, in unison, hatchets swinging, knives slashing. Others had cut the traces and released the mules. More had ridden in and taken the mules and the attackers away.

All of this done in mere seconds.

Briggs didn't know where to start. His stomach seemed ready to explode. He gulped in air as he turned away from the carnage to collect his thoughts. He would have to bury the dead, of course, but now he was so filled with the horror of the slaughter that he couldn't face such a chore. He walked around in a daze, wondering that he had been spared and knowing in his heart that the Cherokee had seen him ride through the gully and had chosen to let him live so that he could witness the massacre and carry its message to others of his race. It was a sobering thought.

Faron looked up at the sky as a shadow crossed his face.

They were already gathering. The smell of blood had brought them, and there they were, one buzzard, two, a third, wheeling overhead, their heads moving from side to side as they glided in circles on silent pinions. The sight of them made the anger inside him boil up and fill him with an almost uncontrollable rage. But there was no enemy close at hand. The Cherokee had left, taking the mules as their booty, and he was alone.

Faron walked back to the first wagon and started looking inside for a shovel. He would bury the dead and ride on to Santa

Fe alone to tell his story to any who would listen. He was just pulling a long-handled shovel from the Willis wagon when he heard the crunch of hooves on sand and rock. He stiffened, started to reach for the butt of his pistol.

"I wouldn't do that if I were you," a man said. "Just turn around real slow and hold your hands out where I can see them."

Faron did as he was told.

There, on a tall horse, sat a tall man, lean as a whip, armed, staring at him from under a wide-brimmed, coal-black hat.

"Mister, maybe you better take a look around before you jump all over any conclusions you already got."

"I saw some Cherokee riding away from here, driving a dozen barebacked mules. I can see what happened. I'm just wondering how you got out from under it."

"I was riding up ahead when it happened. Scouting the trail. I was the wagon master for this bunch of poor souls. And who might you be, stranger?"

"The name's Horatio Blackhawk. And you?"

"Faron Briggs."

"I'll help you bury these folks," Blackhawk said, "and then I'll have a question or two for you."

"What kind of questions?"

"I'm a United States marshal. And I'm hunting a man. A killer. You may have run into him."

"I doubt it."

Blackhawk swung down from his horse.

"You got another shovel?" he asked.

Faron nodded. He looked up as another shadow shrouded his face.

More buzzards were circling. He saw a dozen up there now.

"Try that last wagon there, Marshal. Should be a shovel in there, or hooked to the side."

Blackhawk walked back toward the last wagon, leading his horse.

Faron wondered who the man was looking for. He reminded him, the way he was dressed, the way he walked, of one of those buzzards overhead. Like them, he was hunting a man, but one that was alive, not dead.

"You might as well ask me now," Briggs said.

"Zane. I'm looking for a man named Lew Zane."

"I seen a feller named Lew. He was with another man. Jeff somebody. Can't recall that I heard his last name."

"Do you know if he was headed for Santa Fe?"

"I think they were going to Colorado. Lew and that man he called Jeff."

"Thanks. That's all I needed to know."

The day seemed to darken, although the sun was as bright as a freshly minted twenty-dollar gold piece.

20

The air was thin in Leadville. It lay in the crotch of the Rocky Mountains, two dizzying miles above sea level. Yet Lew had never seen such a small town so full of bustling people. When Jack Hardy rode down Harrison Street, pointing out his favorite places, Lew drank it all in as if he were being introduced to a magical city full of delights and wonders.

"Yonder's Haw Tabor's Opera House," Hardy said, his voice laden with pride, "and oh, there's Cy Allen's Monarch Saloon, where many an elbow has bended, and there's Hyman's Saloon, right next door to Haw Tabor's Opera House. Tabor's the richest man in Leadville, smart as a horse, wily as a fox, old Haw is. Them are his initials, H.A.W., and you'll see him and his lovely wife, Baby Doe, sitting in their box listening to the singing, clapping their hands along with the miners and ne'er-do-wells in the gallery."

Lew gawked like a country yokel seeing the tall buildings of New York for the first time.

"If you want to play some poker, yonder's the Board of Trade Saloon," Hardy said. "Ah, I can hear the chink of chips, the clink of glasses, and a powerful thirst coming on. But first, I must show you my mine and my humble abode. And pay you what I owe you."

Lew was tempted to tell Hardy to forget his debt because he was grateful to have a guide to such a wondrous place where men crossed the street with purposeful strides and women hiked their skirts on the board-walks, and wagons and carts filled the street, all going and coming from somewhere, all industrious, all, seemingly, armed with urgent purpose.

"Hungry?" Jack asked.

"Starved. Must be the altitude."

"It'll give a man hunger. You may have a headache for a few days until you get used to the thin air."

Hardy turned a corner and reined up in front of a small café called Casa Alta. People scurried up and down the street and there was no boardwalk. Lew could smell the food as he wrapped his reins around the hitch rail.

They went inside, walked to an empty table in the corner.

"Umm, smells good," Lew said as he picked up a slate with the day's bill of fare. He looked at the prices and nearly choked.

"It costs dear to eat in this place," he said.

"Mining town prices. Don't worry yourself none. I'm paying for both of us."

"All the food listed here is in a foreign language," Lew said.

Hardy laughed. "Mexican. Don't worry about it none. You'll learn the lingo in no time. Let me order for you."

Lew set the slate down and smiled.

"I hope you let me eat it," he said.

They both laughed.

Lew studied the faces of the people, wondering if any of them knew Carol Smith. Or Wayne, for that matter. He had no idea where Carol lived, but according to Jeff, it was some ways out of town.

The waitress came over.

"Hello, Peggy," Jack said. "This is my friend, Lew. Lew Zane. You treat him nice when he comes in, will you?"

"I sure will, Mr. Hardy. Pleased to meet you, Lew. What'll it be today?"

"Bring us both some of that *carne asada*,

some hot *tortillas, fritas papas,* and hot coffee."

"I'll be right back," she said.

"Her name's Margarita, a Mex gal," Jack said. "But everybody here calls her Peggy. She knows most everybody in town."

"Meaning I can ask her where to find Carol Smith?"

"After you get to know her better, yes."

"I see," Lew said.

The food was delicious. Spicy beef, as tender as any he had tasted, beans, and fried potatoes. Washed down with steaming-hot coffee. Lew filled his belly and Jack paid the bill, stuffed some bills in the pocket of Peggy's apron.

"My friend Lew here will probably be back, Peggy. You treat him right, hear?"

"I will, Mr. Hardy. *Ten cuidado,* eh?"

"Thank you, darling."

They rode on through the town, and Lew gazed at the hillsides where tall scaffolds stretched to large cave holes blasted out of sheer rock and places where trees had been shorn to sink mine shafts deep into the heart of the mountain.

They wound their way up a craggy road, leaving the teeming settlement behind, to come upon wooden shacks, smoke curling from rock chimneys, water flowing in a creek, and a blue pall over the shacks, adding to the mystery of the place. He wondered if Carol lived in any of the cabins, and decided they were all too close to town. Another road, up a steep canyon, and more mines pocking the rugged sides of the mountain, evergreens in staggered phalanxes reaching to the blue sky, and finally, a homely abode nestled in the spruce and pines, where Hardy turned in, a smile on his face.

"Let's tie up to the hitch rail, Lew, and I'll show you my humble dwelling."

The cabin was well made, with whipsawed lumber, a shingled roof with a steep pitch, even a porch, and pine slabs nailed to the sides of every wall.

Inside, Jack left Lew standing in the middle of the front room. Lew noticed that it was nicely furnished, with two divans, plush chairs, one a rocker, some small tables, a desk, oil lamps at strategic places. There were curtains next to the windows that looked to have been made from Mexican blankets, and a footstool near a divan covered in the same colorful material.

Jack returned and handed some bills to Lew.

"As promised," he said.

"I don't know," Lew said. "That's an awful lot of money to rent a horse."

"Take it. If you have to stay awhile and eat at Peggy's café, you'll need it. Now, have a seat and let's talk some business."

Lew took off his hat and sat down in one of the chairs. Hardy sat in the rocker.

"You want a job, Lew?"

"That depends, Jack. I don't know how long I'll be up here. I want to go back to Pueblo. Somewhere in between, I'll need to work."

"Your schedule might work for me. I'm sending another bunch of ore down to Pueblo in a week or two. I'd like you to go with me when I contact a buyer for my silver. He'll pay in cash and I'll need a bodyguard."

"A bodyguard?"

"Honest work. You may not have to do anything. But I'll be packin' quite a bit of cash and I'd like to know I had help in keepin' it."

"Did you have a bodyguard before?"

"Yes," he said, so quickly that Lew got the impression that Hardy didn't want him to pursue the subject. But Lew did anyway.

"What happened to that bodyguard, Jack?"

"Long story. I had made a large sale of silver to a buyer in Santa Fe. My bodyguard had once worked as a constable in Pueblo. He was a good man, I thought. But he was a braggart, and I guess he told some of his police friends about the large amount of money he was guarding. We were staying at a hotel in Pueblo. I had put a large sum in the bank, but still carried a rather large amount with me, intending to take it up to Leadville to pay my workers. The night before we were to leave for Leadville, some armed men broke into my hotel room. They clubbed me senseless, killed the bodyguard, and took all of the money."

"Do you know who it was? Did you see the men who robbed you?" Lew asked.

Hardy nodded.

"I saw them. Filed a complaint with the chief of police. Told him who the men were."

"And what happened?"

"I figure the police all shared in the money that was stolen. Nothing happened. They looked the other way."

"When did this happen?" Lew asked.

"I was on my way back from Pueblo when my horse broke its leg. It just happened. That money is still sitting in the bank down there. I had some that the robbers didn't find. Luckily, I didn't trust my bodyguard completely so the thieves didn't get much, less than a thousand dollars."

"What makes you think I can do any better?"

"You've already had a run-in with one of the men who robbed me," Hardy said.

"I have?"

"I think so. I recognized the ringleader of the gang that broke into my hotel room. Three men. One is a strong-arm who works at the Double Eagle, a man named Ed McDermott. Another was a part-time city constable named Julius Grandy. He had been my bodyguard's partner and I knew him."

"And the third man?"

"Wayne Smith. Wasn't he the one who killed your friend Jeff?"

Lew's palms grew clammy with cold sweat.

"I think so," he said.

"The bodyguard I hired was a man named Abner Casper. When I hired him, he told me a lot about Smith. Smith is an ambitious policeman who is also greedy. Casper said that Smith had a little side business at the Double Eagle. He and a woman named Flora Benitez look for patrons with money who come into her establishment, the Double Eagle, then see to it that they get waylaid when they leave and relieved of their money."

"I heard something like that, too," Lew said.

"But this Smith is greedy, and he's meaner than a snake. The police won't do anything about him, because he's paying them some of his proceeds. I think Smith is graduating from beating up drunks to going after bigger rewards. I think I was one of the first he's robbed because he had confidential information. I think he's planning to do more of the same."

"What do you mean?" Lew asked.

"A lot of the miners here in Leadville are very rich. Some of them are dumb. They go to Pueblo and Santa Fe and buy expensive cigars, play with the painted women, and throw money around to show how rich they are. I think Smith has his eye on some of these jaspers and means to rob every one of them when they sell their silver in Pueblo."

"What makes you think that?"

"Something Casper said when he was dying up in that hotel room."

"I'm listening," Lew said.

"He said Smith had big plans. Smith was going to rob a bunch of men in between Pueblo and Taos, then head for parts unknown. He's just waiting like a damned vulture to pounce on the rich miners who will be heading for Pueblo before the first snow."

"Seems to me, Jack, he means for you to be one of them."

"I know I'm on his list."

"This isn't a job for a lone bodyguard. You'd need an army to go up against Smith and his cronies."

"Maybe not," Hardy said.

He stood up, stretched his arms, and looked out the window.

"In the next few days, Lew, I'm going to meet with every miner I know and lay out a plan for them and for me. We're going to lay a trap for Wayne Smith and his men. I won't give you the details, but I've worked it all out in my mind. We won't get justice from the authorities in Pueblo. We're going to form a vigilance committee."

"Vigilantes?"

"Exactly. But there's something I want you to do, and I'll pay you very well for your services, a bonus if you succeed."

"And what's that, Jack?"

"We stand a better chance if we can cut off the head of the snake. I want you to take on Wayne Smith."

"Kill him?"

"Yes."

"My gun's not for hire," Lew said, and

stood up. "You read me wrong, Jack. I'm not a killer."

Hardy smiled and patted Lew on the back.

"You go on and find Wayne's wife, Lew. She lives way up the canyon you and I rode through to my place. It's another hard ten miles. You'll find her and I think you'll come back and entertain my offer."

"You know Carol Smith? You've known her all this time and never said a word."

"I didn't know who she was until you told me. And I know something else. Something you don't know."

"What's that?"

"Wayne Smith took out a large insurance policy on his wife and his two kids. He plans to come up here and kill them, collect the insurance money. That's why he brought her here and left her all alone."

Lew swore under his breath.

"You can't know all this, Jack. You're just making it up."

"Before I left Pueblo, before we met, I did some checking on Wayne Smith. One of the bankers I know told me about the insurance policy. It's for a very large sum and the word got around in the higher money circles of Pueblo. This Wayne Smith is a snake, a heartless, cold-blooded snake."

Hardy paused and guided Lew to the door.

"Come see me when you've made up your mind, Lew. You can find me here, or up at the mine across the creek, or at the Casa Alta. Just follow the canyon on up, you'll find the lady."

Lew glanced at him when he got to the hitch rail.

"If she's still alive," Hardy said.

21

Shadows began to puddle in the canyon, flow up the evergreens on both sides. Lew felt the air turn chill as the sun fell ever westward. He saw no cabins nor signs of mining after he left Hardy's, although he did see a makeshift shelter on the other side of the creek, long since abandoned by some nameless prospector. And farther along, he began seeing old sluice boxes and dry rockers rotting and weathered, along with rusted airtights strewn along the edge of the creek, and other signs of prospecting, hard living, and broken dreams.

A mule deer darted from the trees in front of him, disappeared in a copse of spruce trees as the echoes from the clattering rocks died away. A feeling of great loneliness came over him as he rode deeper into the mountains. The road grew steeper and Lew struggled to breathe. His head ached, and he wondered if he would have to untie his heavy coat from in back of the cantle once the sun was down and the light gone.

The road grew rougher, rockier, as if the original workers had grown tired and known they could not go much farther. Ruben made a great deal of clatter with his hooves striking the raw stones that lay in his path. Finally, though, Lew realized that they were no longer climbing. The road had leveled off for a long stretch that was fairly straight. The canyon widened, too, and there was more light than before, the sun still hovering somewhere beyond those tall, snow-dusted peaks that jutted to the sky like ancient battlements.

Lew figured he was nearing ten miles traveled along the rugged road, but so rapt had he been in marveling at the country and its trees that he had not kept account of the distance he had come. He had, instead, become homesick, mildly homesick, for the Ozarks hills he had roamed as a boy and young man, the gentleness of them, their openness. Here, he seemed hemmed in by walls of trees so thick he could see no game trails, no open meadows or inviting hollows. As the shadows crept up the mountain, the walls became even more forbidding, and he felt the hostility of trees that clustered so close together and seemed like sentinels barring any from passage into their impenetrable green depths.

The canyon sprawled out, widened to what Lew might call a valley, where sunlight streamed down over a high pass so distant, it seemed more like something painted at the end of the road, unreal, elusive as smoke. And off to his right, he saw another road, hacked through the trees, blasted by dynamite so that it was flanked by two furrows, ditches, which would carry water down to the creek in a time of rain or melting snows.

He followed that road as it wound through the tall, stately pines, the spruce and fir, the juniper, and he saw elk tracks and mule deer spoor crossing the road, leaving marks in the softer places comparatively clear of rocks, as if the animals knew to take the path of least resistance.

Another mile, he figured, perhaps more, and he saw the bare outlines of a manmade structure, nestled deep in the woods, blending in with the natural colors of the trees, but standing out slightly because of its horizontal lines. He rode toward that silent place, wondering if he had found the cabin where Wayne had isolated his wife and children, as remote a place as Lew had ever seen, a prison for one who had no horse or wagon, a prison with green and brown bark bars as thick as a man's trunk.

Smoke spiraled out of the chimney and was torn to wisps in the trees, dissipated in the gentle breeze that wafted aloft. Yet not a sign of life at first glance as the cabin came into full view, small, homely, yet oddly homey in the vastness of the evergreen forest.

The light was fading as he approached the log cabin. The long shadows were drawing up into pools beneath the trees, inky blotches that began to merge and mingle into large black lakes beyond the reach of the last waves of light. He looked around for a stable or barn, but there was only the cabin. It had no porch, nor any outbuildings at all, not even a small shed.

He pulled on the reins and Ruben halted. Jeff's horse stopped alongside. Both horses seemed curious about the cabin, and stared at it with ears stiff and twitching.

"Hello the house," Lew called, and heard his voice swallowed up in the trees. "Anybody to home?"

More silence.

Lew wondered if he had come to the right place, and if he had, whether the woman had gotten someone to take her and her children into town. He waited a few more minutes, then turned his horse, ready to ride out, head for Leadville, and try to find Carol Smith another day.

That's when Lew heard *snick, snick,* the unmistakable sound of two hammerlocks cocking.

He pulled on the reins, felt the bit bite into the back of Ruben's mouth. The horse halted and Lew froze in the saddle, expecting at any moment to hear an explosion marking the last sound he'd ever hear.

"Where'd you get that horse?"

Lew turned and saw the woman holding the shotgun. She stood in front of a large pine tree. Behind her, two small faces peered out from behind that same tree.

"The one I'm riding, ma'am, or the one I'm leading?"

"You know damned well which one I mean. That one with my daddy's saddle on it."

"You must be Carol. Carol Smith."

"So what if I am? You answer my question, mister, and you answer it real quick."

"It's Jeff's horse, all right. He called him Leroy. He's the one who sent me up here to find you."

"Where's my daddy?"

Lew thought over his answer very carefully. If he said the wrong thing, Carol might still shoot him out of the saddle. If he didn't make friends with her right away, he likely never would.

"I can explain everything to you, ma'am, if you'll just put that Greener down and give me the chance."

"How do I know Wayne didn't send you up here?"

"Well, he didn't. I have a message for you from your father. But I can't do anything with my hands up in the air and scared out of my wits that you'll pull those triggers."

"You step down real slow after I come around on your left side. One false move and you'll dance with a load of buckshot in your gizzard."

"Yes'm," Lew said.

"You kids stay right there," she said, and walked around in front of Ruben. She took up a position some ten yards away, then moved the shotgun up and down, indicating for Lew to climb out of the saddle. He did that and stood there, hands over his head.

"Step away from your horse and drop that gunbelt," she said.

"You know, all this is unnecessary, if you'll just —"

She cut him off.

"Do what I say. Won't anybody ever find your miserable body way up here, mister. I

231

don't need much of an excuse to blow you to kingdom come. Now, drop that gunbelt and step well away from it."

Lew unbuckled his belt, swung his pistol out to his side, and let the tip of the holster touch the ground. He lowered his hand and the holster lay flat. He dropped the cartridge belt atop it and took three steps toward her.

"What's the message you got?"

"Just a minute," he said, fishing in his pocket for the note Jeff had written before he died. The money, wrapped in the oilcloth, was in his saddlebags. He hoped he'd be able to deliver both to Carol and she'd put away that lethal double-barreled shotgun.

There wasn't much light left. He held the note out to her, but she shook her head.

"Just drop it on the ground and walk ten paces toward the cabin. Then you stay there while I pick up the note."

"You may not be able to read it in this light," he said.

"Mister, I got eyes like a hawk."

Lew took ten paces and halted. He saw her move toward the note; then her image slipped out of the corner of his eye. He didn't turn his head.

He heard a rustle as she picked up the note. Then silence as she read it.

"You're Lew Zane?"

"I am."

"What happened to my daddy?" she asked.

"It's a long story, Mrs. Smith. And I've come a long way."

"Of course. I'm sorry. We should go inside where we can talk. I'll fetch my children. You can put up the horses out back. Were you bringing Daddy's horse to me, as well?"

"I was, yes."

"Children. Come, children. Inside."

Carol scurried off, her children running to catch up to her. Lew walked back, picked up his gunbelt. He strapped it on, buckled it, and then led the two horses in back of the cabin. There was a lean-to built onto the cabin, but no sign that any stock had inhabited it in some time. There was a feed trough and a water barrel, cut in half, some pegs to hang tack, and a crude sawhorse that would accommodate a couple of saddles. It was small, efficient, and Lew stripped the horses, poured some grain into the bin, what was left in his and Jeff's saddlebags, and looked around for a well. He did not see one in the darkness, but poured water from two canteens into the dry barrel. He hefted the saddlebags, drew his rifle from its sheath, shouldered it, and went back around the front and knocked on the door.

He heard the latch lift and the door opened. He saw two lamps shimmering on tables inside, filling the room with a golden glow. There was no fire in the hearth, but the lamps gave off plenty of light.

"I see you're wearing your pistol again, Mr. Zane. And carrying a rifle. I'm still not sure who you are."

"Yes'm. Please call me Lew. And I wear my pistol because it's part of my dress. And I brought my rifle in by way of habit. Your father's rifle is still outside, and I'll bring it in out of the weather, if you wish."

"Yes, later. I want to hear about my father. First, these are my children, Keith, who is twelve, and Lynn, who's ten. We call her Lynnie."

"Hello," Lew said.

"Now, children, go in your bedroom and read quietly. I want to talk to Mr. Zane. Will you be good?"

"Yes, Mama," the children chorused, and then dashed into a room, closed the door.

Lew set down the saddlebags and his rifle, sat in a chair facing the small worn divan. Carol sat on the divan, watched as he rummaged through one of the saddlebags. He pulled out the oilskin packet, handed it to her. Then, he reached in his pocket and pulled out three one-hundred-dollar bills.

He handed these to her, as well.

"The money in the oilskin pouch is some your father asked me to give you. The other money came from renting his horse to a man I met who was afoot."

She opened the packet, plucked out the money.

"All this money," she said. "For me?"

"Yes, it's all yours, and your father's horse, saddle, and bridle. All he had with him when he died."

She went silent, and then glanced at the note. She read it and then doubled over, tears streaming from her eyes, trickling down her face.

"It's true, then," she said. "My daddy's dead?"

"Yes."

"That poor man. Coming all the way out here to see me. I hope he passed away quietly, without any pain. How did he die?"

Lew told her, leaving nothing out, until he came to the very end.

"Your father didn't die from the bullet the doctor pulled out of him, Mrs. Smith."

"It's Carol, please."

"Carol, I believe your husband Wayne came up to the room and strangled Jeff with his bare hands."

"Wayne? Oh, no. He couldn't."

He told her about the Double Eagle and how he believed Wayne had waited to ambush them. He told about being knocked out, the room keys taken from him, and then finding her father dead, strangled to death.

And then, he told her what he had learned from Jack Hardy on the ride up to Leadville.

"Your husband plans to kill you and your two children to collect the money on an insurance policy he took out in your name."

Carol's face drained of color, turned ashen. Lamplight played on her face. She seemed to age before his eyes, just for a brief moment as she took a breath and tried to recover from the shock of his revelation.

"I knew Wayne was no damned good," she said, a bitter edge to her voice, "but I didn't think he would stoop to murdering my father, and harming his own children."

"And you, Carol," Lew said softly. "You are in grave danger. That's another reason I wear this pistol and carry that rifle. You said in your letter that a man came up here and you had to drive him away. Has he given you any more trouble?"

"I see him every so often. That's why I carry that shotgun around when I'm outside. I'm afraid of him."

"What is his name, may I ask?"

"His name is Don McDermott."

Lew sucked in a breath through his nostrils. Ed McDermott was the burly man in the Double Eagle who had thrown him and Jeff out. Could he be the brother of Don McDermott?

"When did you last see this McDermott?" Lew asked.

"It's been a few days. Nearly a week, I think. When I heard your horse, the horses, I thought that was Don coming back up here. That's why I went outside and hid with my children."

"So he could come back at any time."

"Yes. At least once a week. And we're nearly out of food. He knows that. He says he has food for me, but I don't trust him."

Perhaps, Lew thought, Don was meant to be Carol's assassin. If so, she was in even more danger than he realized, or than she realized. And now that he was in the picture, McDermott might make his move at any time.

Carol looked at Lew and he saw it in her eyes. Just a flicker, but it was there.

Fear.

And her look turned his heart cold.

22

Lew excused himself while Carol absorbed all that he had told her. He went back to the lean-to and hobbled the horses, just in case they wanted to wander, saw that they had nibbled at the grain and sipped some water. He did all this by feel since by then it was pitch dark and the moon had not yet risen.

Back inside, Lew opened his and Jeff's saddlebags.

"You said you were short of food, Carol. I have some staples here which might come in handy."

"I have venison," she said. "There's plenty of game around and I'm a good shot. Daddy taught me to hunt and fish when I was a girl back in Bolivar."

Lew laid out the staples still stored in the saddlebags: flour, salt, sugar, beans, and coffee. Carol's eyes widened like a child's at Christmas and she clapped her hands together.

"Oh, you're a godsend, Lew Zane. The very things I was running low on, and you come with them. I feel rich, richer than the money makes me feel."

She began to gather up the foodstuffs and called to her children, who came rushing out of their room. Their eyes, too, widened at the sight of food, and Lew wished he had some candies for them, but he had none.

"I'll cook the beans tomorrow," Carol said, "but tonight we'll have a stew I made this morning with the last of the potatoes and leeks. And we can have coffee, which I've not tasted in weeks, and I'll make sugar cookies from the flour you gave us."

"Where is your stove?" Lew asked.

She pointed to the hearth. "That's where I cook the stews and broths I make, but I have a small oven in the back room where I can bake and heat water to boiling. It's the smallest stove I've ever seen. Keith calls it a midget stove and Lynnie, she says it's a stove used by the fairies. Oh, these children. What imaginations they have."

Lew watched Carol, delighting in her chatter. Her soft Missouri accent reminded him of home. She was a few years older than he, but he remembered she had gotten married while very young. She still had a girlish quality, at least the way she looked, with her soft brown hair, blue eyes, dimples, a firm, lithe figure. She didn't remind him of Seneca except in an odd way. She was a young woman and she was from Missouri. He felt at home with her.

As he watched Carol rushing to get supper on the table, and listened to the small sweet voices of the children, he thought how lucky he was to be in that place, with this little family. He realized that Carol was exerting herself just to keep her mind off of the terrible things he had told her. He knew she was grieving for her father, but also mourning the horror of her marriage. Wayne had made her a prisoner and now was planning to murder her. Yet there was Carol, smiling, laughing, chattering with her children, as if she hadn't a care in the world.

They sat down to a warm supper of venison stew. Carol had made biscuits, and there was a fire in the hearth. Carol intoned a simple prayer of gratitude for the food while the children bowed their heads over folded hands. There was a candle in the center of the table, giving off a glow of celebration even under such homely conditions and with such meager fare.

"I thought we'd have coffee afterwards," she said, "when Keith and Lynnie have gone to sleep."

"This is a fine meal, Carol."

"Why, thank you, Lew. And thanks to you."

"Mama," Keith said, "is this man our hero?"

Carol blushed. Lynn flashed a snaggle-toothed grin.

"Keith, little people should be seen and not heard."

"But you said Mr. Lew was our hero. Didn't she, Lynnie?"

"Yes, Mama," Lynn said. "You told us."

"Shhh," Carol said, still blushing. She turned to Lew. "I've been telling them that one day a hero would ride up here and help us. I told them it would probably be their father, but as time went on, and they kept asking me when our hero would come, I told them it might not be their father. It might be anybody."

"Tonight, you said it was Mr. Lew," Keith said. "That he was our hero."

"Forgive me, Lew. I guess I did say that."

"It's all right. I believe in heroes, too. Did you ever read Homer?"

She shook her head.

"Who was Homer?" Keith asked.

"He was a writer who lived a long time ago, maybe twenty-five hundred years ago,

241

and he wrote about heroes."

"Are you a hero, Mr. Lew?" Lynn asked.

Lew shook his head. "I don't think so. Heroes are big people with special powers."

"To us," Carol said, "you are a hero. Now, you children be quiet and let Lew eat. And you, both of you, finish your supper."

"Yes, ma'am," both children said in unison. But they kept looking up at Lew, who winked at them when their mother wasn't looking.

When they were finished, Lew helped her clean up. She washed the dishes and he dried them. She checked on the children to see if they were asleep, then put the water on to boil for their coffee. The aroma permeated the cabin and added to Lew's feeling of being at home. They sat in the living room with the fire in the hearth burning down low.

"I wish I had had time to bake a pie, although I have no fruit."

"Jeff — ah, your father and I ate the last of the peaches before we got to Pueblo and I didn't think to buy any more."

"Don McDermott kept telling me he had peaches and pears for me in airtights, but of course I wouldn't let him come up to the cabin."

"You did the best thing, keeping him

away," Lew said. "I've been thinking about that man and his offers to you."

"Oh? And what have you decided about him?"

"He's a liar," Lew said. "If he was really bringing you groceries and such, all he had to do was leave it at the end of the lane and ride on back down to Leadville."

"I never thought of that," she said.

"McDermott wanted to gain your trust so when it came time to, ah, to get rid of you, it would be easy. If he really cared about you and the children, he would have brought food to you and left it, no questions asked."

"You know, I think you're right."

"Good coffee," he said, and took another sip. He looked at Carol over the rim and wondered what was going on in her mind. She showed no sign that she was upset over her husband's scheme to murder her in order to collect insurance money. But he knew she had to be concerned.

"You'll have to stay the night," she said. "I'm sorry that we have only one bed, for me and the children. It'll get too cold for you to sleep outside."

"I have a bedroll out in the lean-to," he said.

"Why didn't you bring it in?" she asked.

"I didn't want to overstep my bounds."

She laughed. "Why, that's just silly. If you tried to ride back down that canyon in the dark, you'd liable to break your horse's leg, maybe get thrown. There's mountain lions and bears up here and the lions prowl at night. They aren't afraid to attack a horse or a man."

"I'll keep that in mind."

He changed the subject.

"What are you going to do, Carol? What do you want to do?"

"I can't stay here," she said. "I can't stay anywhere. I suppose I should go to the police and tell them what Wayne plans to do."

"Be hard to prove."

"Yes, I know. I don't know what to do. Do you have any suggestions?"

He drew a breath and looked at her, wondering what he could do for her, if anything. She was in a bad spot. She had no way to get to town, even with the money she now had. And her life was in danger, no matter where she went. As long as Don Mc-Dermott was watching her, she was in grave danger. And if she went to Pueblo, that's where Wayne was, and the danger was even greater.

"I made a friend in Leadville, Carol. Tomorrow, you and the kids can ride down there with me. He'll be able to help me find a safe place for you and the children."

She sighed.

"I'd do anything to get out of this prison," she said.

He finished his coffee, stood up.

"I'll bring my bedroll in, lay out here in front of the fire."

"That'll be fine," she said. "I'm tired. I'll say good night now. I hope you can get a good night's sleep on that hard floor."

Lew laughed.

"I've slept in worse places."

He walked outside and looked up at the stars. The moon was up, and it sailed high over the mountain peaks. He could see only a small part of the sky through the pines that stretched so high into the darkness.

He walked around back, wishing he had brought a lantern. But he knew the bedroll was still tied on his saddle and he could find it in the dark. He stood there a moment, breathing in the scent of spruce and pine, the fragrance of the fir trees. He was still giddy from the thin air, but the meal had helped and his headache was gone.

He untied the thongs that held his bedroll, and then walked over to Jeff's saddle and jerked his rifle from its scabbard. He had started walking toward the front of the cabin when he heard a scrape that brought him up short. He stood there, hugging the side of the cabin, listening. What he had heard sounded like an animal's hoof scraping against a loose stone. A hoof or a boot.

In the clear mountain air, sound carried a long way, but this had sounded close. Lew didn't make a move, but stood there like a statue, his ears attuned to the slightest noise.

Then, he heard it again. Not a scrape this time, but the unmistakable crunch of a boot on gravel. Just that, and nothing more.

Lew eased down into a crouch. He took the bedroll from his shoulder and set it down. He grabbed the lever of Jeff's rifle, ready to cock it.

He tried to pinpoint exactly where he had heard the last sound. It came from in front of the cabin, down the lane that led up from the canyon floor. What had he heard? A man? A deer? A bear? He held his breath, tried not to shiver in the chill night air.

Crunch, crunch, snap. Then, "Shhh."

Two men, Lew decided, and they couldn't be more than fifty yards from him, heading toward the cabin. He crept up to the front edge of the wall. Lamplight flooded through the front window, but only splashed a yard or two. Beyond was darkness. Then he heard more footsteps. He levered a cartridge into the chamber of Jeff's rifle and started looking for a target.

"Damnit, Pete, be quiet." A loud whisper.

"That wasn't me. I tell you, Don, somebody's up there 'sides that woman and her kids."

"Shut your damned mouth."

Then, Lew heard a branch snap somewhere off to his right.

He cursed silently. There were at least three men.

The night exploded with the loud thunder of a rifle. He saw a blossom of orange flame and heard the sizzle of a bullet crease the air just over his head and slam into the log just above where he crouched. Splinters showered down on him, stinging the side of his face just at the hairline.

He saw a dark shape just beyond the afterimage of the muzzle flash and whirled, swinging his rifle from the hip.

From inside the house, Lew heard a scream.

A scream of terror that turned his blood to cold jelly.

23

Lew fired his rifle from the hip, then threw himself headlong to the ground. He twisted sideways to lever another shell into the firing chamber. Rifles opened up, smearing the night with orange and red flame. Bullets plowed furrows all around him. He heard a grunt and knew his bullet had found a human target, but the man to his right fired another round that fried the air over his head.

He shot at a shadowy figure running across the road, and heard the bullet strike a rock and ricochet off into the dark with a high-pitched whine. He knew he was in a bad spot and rolled toward the nearest tree. Another shot, and a bullet thudded into one of the logs on the front of the cabin.

"Get him," a voice shouted, and two rifles opened up, firing at the place where Lew had lain seconds before.

Lew fired at one of the shooters and saw

him go down. He stood up, sealing himself against a pine while he worked the lever on Jeff's rifle. He had to be sparing with his shots because all the firepower he had was what was in the magazine.

A bullet struck the tree where Lew was standing. He dashed to another and drew more fire. He threw down on the muzzle flash and fired where he thought the shooter would be. He heard a loud smack and then a crash. He looked out and saw another man go down.

He jacked another shell into the chamber and waited.

No one shot at him, and he could hear his own breathing in the silence.

Then he heard the crunch of a foot. Someone was moving toward the cabin. He hoped Carol would sit tight and keep her shotgun handy in case anyone got past him and broke in.

"I'm hit," a man called out, and Lew detected pain in his voice.

Lew hugged the tree, listening to the rustlings in the woods. The sounds were close by, and from the crunchings and snappings, he knew one of the men was trying to circle him and attack his right flank, where he was exposed.

One man was down, he figured. Probably

another was wounded, but still able to move. The third man could be the one coming up on his flank. He leaned the rifle against the pine tree and drew his pistol.

Another sound off to his left. Two men were approaching now, one on either flank. If he stayed there, he'd be cut down, with attackers on both sides.

He breathed deep, trying to think.

More crunching, softer this time, as if someone were creeping toward him, trying not to make noise.

Lew wanted them close, but he also wanted the advantage.

He hunkered down into a squat, trying to minimize his silhouette. The two men knew where he was and they were closing in. Lew waited, holding his breath.

The rustle of leaves off to his right. Closer now. He knew that if he did not move, either man would have a hard time seeing just where he was. He held his Colt at the ready, straining his ears to pick up any scrap of sound. The whisper of a foot grazing the ground. The soft crunch of earth as the man put his weight on the foot. Lew did not move. He was staring straight into darkness, but he was looking in the direction of the sounds off to his right.

Silence from inside the cabin.

More movement. This time to his left. Closer than before.

Lew squinted, peering into the darkness of the woods, seeking out any movement, any shape that was not natural. His eyes played tricks on him. He saw men all around him until he realized they were trees. Every shadow looked ominous. Neither man was moving. They were, like Lew, waiting. Listening.

Lew put his thumb on the hammer of his pistol. At the same time, he gently squeezed the trigger, ticking it back a short distance until he felt the tension, the resistance. Then he thumbed the hammer down. There was a soft click, but so muted he himself could barely hear it. By pulling on the trigger slightly, he avoided the loud metallic snick of the mechanism engaging the sear.

Now, he was ready.

And he knew it would not be long. One of the men would lose patience. Which one? He did not know. But the man on his right was closer. He could be the one who shot first.

Lew felt himself relax. He was ready. He batted his eyelids to clear his vision. He breathed very slowly, evenly.

The waiting, nevertheless, was agony.

Moments ticked by. The silence deepened.

Then, a small scrape as something moved off to his right. He saw a pine tree expand, broaden its trunk. A shadow within a shadow. A tree growing larger, low down. A man sliding away from the tree, ready to take a shot.

Lew fixed the growing shadow in his mind, locked onto it with his keen eyesight. He brought the pistol up as if it weighed a hundred pounds. Slow and even, like a foot coming out of quicksand.

He leveled his pistol at the shadow.

Then the shadow broke its connection to the tree. Just enough to present Lew with a silhouette.

He fired, squeezing the trigger as he held his breath. The pistol roared, bucked in his hand. Sparks and flame spewed from the muzzle, and he thought he heard the bullet sizzle through the air like an angry bee. He cocked the pistol again as the bullet smacked home, striking flesh, cracking ribs.

"Aaaah." The sound of a man struck in the chest, expelling air from his lungs.

Lew slid around the tree to the opposite side as he heard the man fall headlong, crashing into twigs, pine needles, rocks.

He looked off to his left, ready to fire.

There was more noise, a scrambling, then footsteps running away. Down the road toward the creek. Lew peered out from behind the tree and saw the dark figure of a man before the image merged into the dark shadows and disappeared.

Lew waited, listening for any more sounds of movement. The man he had dropped, off to his right, was probably no longer breathing. Lew could detect no sign of life. Nor of the first man he had shot. He didn't know where the man was, exactly, but he knew he was down and either dead or dying.

Moments passed before Lew rose to his feet. He kept his pistol at the ready, walked over to the last man he had shot. The man was lying facedown, his rifle by his side. Lew stuck the tip of his boot under the man's belly, kicked upward, and turned him over. There was a bullet hole in his chest. A lot of blood on his belly. The man was not breathing.

Lew started to look for the first man, wary, staying to a crouch, just in case there was still life and danger there.

He found him a few yards in from the clearing, between two trees. He lay on his side, his arms outstretched, as if trying to reach for some last bit of life. Lew touched him with his boot and pushed until the man lay flat on his back. This man, too, was dead. There was blood across his abdomen and on his mouth and chin. He could not see the bullet hole in the darkness.

Lew walked a wide circle around the cabin, stopping every so often to listen. A few moments before, he had heard hoofbeats down on the road. They had faded into a deep silence that lingered still.

When Lew had completed his rounds, he retrieved Jeff's rifle and walked up to the cabin, eased the door open.

"It's just me, Carol," he called out before he entered. "All clear."

He heard the muffled whispers of the children, then Carol trying to soothe them, calm them down. He closed the front door, dropped the latch, and stood there, waiting, listening.

Finally, Carol appeared, the shotgun in her hands. She was wearing a pale pink nightgown and her hair was tousled. There were shadows under her eyes.

"Lew what happened out there? Are you all right?"

"Light a lantern," he said. "And come with me. I want you to look at something."

She hesitated.

"It's important," he said. "You won't need the shotgun. This is your daddy's rifle, by the way."

"I recognize it," she said. "I'll be just a

minute."

Lew waited. Finally, Carol reappeared wearing a cotton dress and a sweater. She held a lighted lantern in her hand. The two walked outside.

"Where are you taking me?" she asked.

"It's gruesome, but it has to be done. I want you to look at these men out in the woods."

"What men?"

"Dead men."

Carol gasped, but walked on, trying to keep up with Lew's long stride.

When she saw the man lying on his back, she held the lantern up so that it would shed more light on him.

"Is he dead?"

"Yes."

They walked over to the man. Carol stared down at him. She did not turn away, as Lew would have thought.

"Do you recognize him, Carol? Is this Don McDermott?"

"No, it's not Don McDermott. And I don't recognize him. Who is he?"

"I don't know. Come, there's another one you have to see."

They walked over to the other dead man. Again, Carol held the lantern up over her head. She looked at the man, then shook her head.

"This isn't Don McDermott, either. I don't know who this man is. Or was."

"Then maybe McDermott is the man who got away."

"There were three of them?"

"Yes, and I think they came up here to kill you and your children."

She shuddered and shrank against Lew. He put an arm around her shoulder until the spasm passed.

"Lew, this is frightening."

"I know. It's lucky I was here, maybe."

"No maybe about it. Oh, I might have held them off. But three men. How could Wayne do something like this to me? And to his children?"

"Money makes men do terrible things sometimes."

"I thought Wayne loved me. He did once, I think. We — when we got married I was only seventeen. I thought it was forever."

"Greed is a terrible thing, Carol."

She shuddered again. "I'm trying to understand what's in that mind of his. I know he liked money, and I knew he was involved in something illegal. But he never talked about it. He never told me what he was going to do. When he brought me here, he made me think he'd be gone for only a few days. I haven't seen him since. He — he gave me no warning."

"Let's go back inside. I'm sorry I had to do this to you, but I had to know. If McDermott was the man who got away, then he knows what you look like. If you go back to Leadville, he'll be waiting for you."

"What am I going to do?"

"Let me take care of it. Look, you get some sleep. I'll bury these men in shallow graves, report their deaths. Tomorrow, we'll ride out of here and I'll take you to a safe place."

"Oh, Lew," she said as they walked back toward the cabin, "I don't know what I would have done if you hadn't come along."

"I expect," he said, "you would have survived. You're a hero, too."

"What?"

"A hero isn't always a man, you know. Many a strong woman has been a hero, in history, in literature."

"Maybe I ought to read those books you talked about to the children."

"They would do you no harm," he said.

Lew found a shovel in the lean-to. He dragged the dead men well away from the cabin and dug shallow graves for them. He stripped them of guns and money, covered them with dirt and rocks. When he was finished, he stood off a ways and looked up at the starry sky. He heard a wolf howl somewhere up the mountain. It was a lonesome sound and sent shivers up his spine.

It sounded, he thought, like a lost soul. And maybe it was.

24

Seneca called out to him. Her voice was a faraway whisper, so soft he could barely hear it, and then he saw her standing behind a waterfall, naked, her skin shimmering with the silvery sheen of cascading water. Behind her, a dark cave and the heady scent of lilacs floating on the air, a seductive perfume that lured him toward a rippling pool beneath a craggy mountain. Then, the muffled cough of a mountain lion, and he saw it wending its way along the gilded rimrock just above the waterfall, its hide as tawny as a field of wheat on a golden morning in summer, its muscles rippling with each careful step, its black-tipped tail twitching as it closed on its prey. Then, the cougar leaped from the ledge, dove down through the waterfall straight at Seneca. She looked up and called his name again softly; again and again she called his name, and he broke out of the dream in a cold sweat as the dark pool filled with flowers and their smothering scent came to him in a sudden rush of an airless wind.

"Lew, Lew," Carol said. "Time to get up, I think."

Lew opened his eyes and saw her kneeling next to his bedroll, her knee pushing through the fold of the dress that buttoned down the front. She had her hand on his shoulder and was rocking him. She smelled of lilac water and pine, of hyacinth and spruce, of fresh-cut fir and fragrant loam.

"Carol?"

"Yes, you silly. Who did you think it was? It's morning and the sun is up. I have something to show you, you lazy boy."

Lew sat up, rubbed his eyes. They were rimmed with the sand of sleep, gritty under his fingertips.

"Oh, boy, I really slept."

"Yes, you did."

She stood up and looked down at him. Lew looked around the room, seeing it for the first time in daylight. Sun streamed through the windows and he tasted the fresh mountain air as if she had opened the door to let the morning inside. He got to his feet and felt the stiffness in his muscles, his bones. There were tender spots on his shoulder blades from sleeping on the hard floor, and his feet seemed unaccustomed to being bootless. He wiggled his toes and picked up his boots, crabbed to the divan, sat down, and pulled them on. His gamy smell fought with the aroma of lilacs and pine, with all the other scents of a mountain morning.

"Is it late?" he asked her.

"No, not late, but you asked me to awaken you if we were up before you. And we were. I've made a sort of breakfast for us, biscuits with venison gravy and sliced deer meat and — ."

"And coffee," he said. "I can smell it now."

"Come," she said. "I want you to look outside, at the mountains on the other side of the canyon."

Lew followed Carol to the front door. She opened it and stepped outside. Lew went out and stood beside her. They both stared at the mountain peaks beyond the canyon floor.

"Beautiful," Lew said.

There was a fresh mantle of snow on the high peaks.

"It looks so pure," she said.

"Yes. I've never seen anything like it."

"The next snow could come at any time, Lew. If it snowed down here tonight, we could be stuck here all winter. I wonder if that's what Wayne wanted to happen to us."

"No, I think he wasn't relying on snow to keep you up here. That's why those men paid us a visit last night. Wayne wants something more permanent than a snow-fall."

"It's still hard for me to believe he would do such a thing."

"Even after last night?"

"Yes. Even after that."

They ate breakfast, but Lew was nervous. He kept listening to every little sound, half-expecting Don McDermott to come riding up to the cabin, guns blazing. When they had finished eating and the dishes were washed and put away, Lew told Carol that it was time to leave.

"Just take with you what you really want and need, Carol. You and Lynnie can ride your father's horse. I'll take Keith with me. We probably won't be able to carry all that you might want."

"With the money you gave me, I can buy what we need. I just want to get away from this place."

"We could run into McDermott on the way down the canyon, you know. You'll have to carry your daddy's rifle across your lap. That or the Greener."

"The rifle," she said. "I've shot it many

times before back home."

In less than an hour, Lew, Carol, and the children were saddled up and riding down the lane to the road. Lew led the way, his rifle across the pommel, a cartridge in the chamber, the hammer on half-cock. The kids and Carol kept looking up at the newly fallen snow, but Lew was reading tracks, watching the road ahead, looking for any signs of an ambush.

They had traveled the ten miles or so without incident when Lew turned into Jack Hardy's cabin. He had been hearing distant blasts all morning on the ride down, and now the sounds were closer. It seemed to him that the ground shook every time someone touched off the dynamite to blast through the rock in search of silver.

"What is this place?" Carol asked as Lew reined to a halt.

"A man who might help us lives here. I hope he's home."

He looked across the canyon and up the slope. The open maw of Jack's Little Nellie Mine looked vacant and quiet.

"Jack, you home?" Lew called.

The door of the shack opened and Jack stood there, shirtless, his grizzled face covered in soapy lather.

"I see you found the gal and her kids, Lew.

Light down. Got a lot to tell you. Come on and make yourselves to home. I'll finish scraping my face out back and we can chew the fat."

Carol hesitated when Lew swung down and hefted Keith to the ground.

"What's the matter?" he asked.

"I — I guess I'm a little scared. I don't know that man."

"He's a friend. There's nothing to worry about. I'm hoping he'll know where I can hide you out, where you'll be safe, until this business is over."

"You mean McDermott?" she said.

"I mean McDermott and your husband."

"But . . ."

"Or you can take your chances with Wayne, Carol. Whatever you decide."

Lew walked over and held out his arms for Lynn.

"It's all right, Lynnie. We'll stop here for a while."

Lynn beamed and held out her arms. She fell into Lew's arms, and he gave her a little swing in a half circle before he set her feet down.

"Was that fun?" he asked.

"Yes. Do it again, Mr. Lew."

"Some other time," he said, then helped Carol out of the saddle. They all walked to the shack and went inside.

Carol released a sigh of admiration when she saw the polished knotty-pine interior of the shack, the hardwood floors, the large table in the center of the room, surrounded by several well-made, high-backed chairs. Along the walls, there were comfortable sofas and chairs, footstools, small tables with huge clay ashtrays. There was a candle chandelier hanging from a ceiling beam and several Aladdin lamps sitting in wall inlays. There was a bookcase and a framed wall map of Pueblo, Salida, and Leadville. The room smelled of cherrywood and pine. The cedar-topped table gleamed with polish, its surface clean and free of dust.

It was obvious to Lew that Hardy was no ordinary miner. Lew could still smell the faint odor of cigar smoke and whiskey as he gazed at a cherrywood cabinet at the far end of the room, its doors slightly open, revealing bottles of expensive whiskey, rye and scotch.

"Be right out," Hardy called from the back of the shack that was so homely outside, so elegant inside.

Carol put the children on a divan and sat in one of the easy chairs. Lew stood there, studying the map, tracing Fountain Creek and the Arkansas River near Pueblo with the tip of his finger. It was a relief map, showing the mountains and some of the prairie east of Pueblo. Arrows on the map pointed toward Denver to the north and Santa Fe to the south.

Hardy entered the room, dressed in clean clothes, shined boots, his hair combed, beard trimmed. He smelled of rosewater and he was smiling.

"Glad you got down here, Lew. We've made progress. And who do we have here?"

Lew introduced Carol and her children, Keith and Lynn. He told Hardy what had happened the night before, and that he suspected Don McDermott was the man who got away.

"I know McDermott," Hardy said. "He's one of the hardcases who have been accused of everything from claim jumping to public brawling. The two men you killed were probably Pete Mortimer and Willy Connelly, who have pasts shadier than McDermott's. Good riddance."

"I believe Carol is still in danger, Jack. I thought you might have some ideas on where she and her children could stay where they'd be safe."

Hardy sat down in one of the chairs. He waved to an empty sofa as he looked at Lew. Lew sat down, leaned forward to hear what

Jack had to say.

"We had a long meeting last night right here," Hardy said. "Mine owners I respect and trust. No police, who have already proven to us that they take bribes and are probably in cahoots with the brigands and highwaymen we'll face when we leave Leadville."

Lew and Carol exchanged glances.

"Tomorrow, all of us are taking our ore down to Pueblo. Several wagons. Lots of armed men. We don't believe anyone will attack us for the ore. But in a few weeks, we'll all be going to Santa Fe to sell our silver, and that's when we think Wayne Smith will try and rob us. We're not going to wait for that to happen."

"What are you going to do?" Lew asked.

"We're going to display several strongboxes full of silver in Pueblo's town square. We're going to load those on several wagons and tell everyone we're heading for Santa Fe. Then, before that wagon leaves, the strongboxes full of silver will be replaced with empty strongboxes.

"There will be two men sitting on the buckboards of each covered wagon. Inside each wagon will be more armed men, hidden from view. We think Smith and his men will attack us somewhere near Spanish

Peaks. We'll be ready for them. What do you think of this plan, Lew?"

Lew looked over at Carol, who seemed lost in thought. She had a dreamy look on her face, as if she had been drugged. There was a vacancy to her eyes.

"I don't think much of your plan, Jack. I think Wayne Smith is probably too smart to think you'd show all that silver and then carry it out of town, no matter how many armed men you have with you."

"Well, that's what he's done before, robbed some of us right around Spanish Peaks. Plenty of cover, a long way from help."

Lew thought about Pope and Canby. If he had not gone after them, they would have gotten away with three murders.

"The best defense," Lew said, "is a good offense."

"What?" Jack said.

"If you know where a nest of snakes is, you don't just walk by it with a big stick. You go into the nest with shotguns and clean out the snakes. Then you can walk there anytime you want."

"You think we ought to go after Smith and his men before they try anything?"

"You already said they got away with this before. Yes, go after them, like I'm going after Don McDermott. You don't wait for snakes to strike, Jack. You kill them before they can sink their poisonous teeth into your leg."

Carol smiled at Lew. It was a wan smile, but a smile of approval.

"I don't think we can do that," Jack said. "I don't think the other mine owners will want to take the law into their own hands. Certainly not under the very eyes of the law in Pueblo."

"Then, you're going to lose, Jack. You'll lose some men, surely, and you may wind up losing everything."

Silence filled the room. Jack leaned back and stared up at the ceiling.

Lew took a breath and looked at Carol, then at her children.

He still didn't know where they would be safe, and Jack had not offered any suggestions. But something Jack had said had given Lew an idea. It was risky, but it might work. At least his idea had a better chance of success than Jack's, which involved a lot of armed men waiting to be attacked.

For the time being, though, Lew vowed to keep his thoughts to himself. Too many people already knew about Jack's plan. Some might talk once they got some liquor inside them, drank some bravery, and began to brag.

No, he would not say anything to anyone. What he would do, he would do alone.

And if he failed, there would be no one to blame except himself.

25

Lew stood up, looked directly at Jack Hardy.

"Will you do me a favor, Jack?"

"If I can."

"I'd like to leave Carol and the kids here while I ride into Leadville, look for a place where they can stay. I won't be long. No more than two hours."

Carol opened her mouth to protest, but Lew held up a hand, pushed it toward her.

"I have to meet some friends in town at noon," Jack said. "I suppose they could stay here with me. But no more than two hours at the most."

"All right," Lew said. "Carol, I'll be back for you and the children."

"I just hate to impose on Mr. Hardy," she said.

Hardy said nothing. Lew could see that he didn't like to be saddled with a woman and two children. But he would sit still for it. That was good enough for Lew, who started for the door.

"I'll be back in two hours," he said before anyone could think too much about what he had done.

Leadville was teeming with activity as people started heading out of town with their wagons loaded. The air was crisp and the day sunny, but that snowfall on the high peaks the night before had spooked a lot of people who didn't want to be trapped in Leadville for the winter.

Lew rode down Harrison Street and then turned on to a side street. He was looking for a particular kind of place and he knew he didn't have much time. At the edge of town, he saw a small house with a wagon and two mules in front of it. It sat by itself at the edge of a small creek. A man and a woman were carrying out boxes and carpet-bags, loading them into the open wagon. A small boy carried a sack of wooden toys out the door. Lew rode up to the man.

"A minute of your time, sir," he said.

"Make it quick. I'm in a hurry."

"Do you own this place?"

"Yeah, I own it, why?"

"You're leaving, am I right?"

"What in hell does it look like? Winter's a-comin' and we're heading for Santa Fe."

"I'd like to rent your house from you. Just

for a few days."

The woman walked over. The little boy was trying to lift his sack up into the wagon. His arms were too short. He made little short hops to no avail. To Lew, he looked like a life-sized jumping jack.

"What's this all about, Harvey?" the woman asked.

"Ruthie, it's no concern of your'n. Help the boy with his sack yonder."

"Did I hear this man say he wanted to pay us money to rent our place?"

"Yes, ma'am, I would like to rent your house for a few days."

"It's going to snow, you know," Harvey said. "That's why we're leaving."

"I know," Lew said. "I'm leaving, too, but I've got a wife and kids and no place to stay until we're ready to leave."

"A wife and kids, you say? Harvey, listen to the man." The woman, a red-haired, brown-eyed woman of Amazonian stature, stood eye-to-eye with Harvey, who was not a small man by any means.

"I'm listening, Ruthie. If you'd just leave us talk."

"I'll pay you for a week's rent," Lew said. "Whatever you're asking. We'll leave the place clean as we find it and lock it up tight when we go."

The man moved his hat to one side and scratched his head as if he was actually pondering his decision. Lew figured he had already made up his mind.

"Well, now," Harvey said. "A whole week. And what if you get snowed in and can't get out until the spring?"

"Tell him about snowshoes, Harvey. They's two sets hangin' in the back storeroom." Ruth Lee grabbed the sack from her son's hands and heaved it onto the wagon. The little boy started to whimper.

"I'll get out in a week," Lew said. "One way or another. Might only need it for a couple of days, though."

"Don't bet on the weather up here, son," Harvey said. "It'll get you every time."

"Harvey, it's fifty dollars a day, three hundred and fifty dollars the week."

"That much?" Lew said, looking at Harvey, whose lips began to twist into a knot as he squinched his eyes to a pair of slits, as if he were in pain.

"Son, I've seen rents on places like mine go for better'n five hunnert dollars a day in the boom. And ain't nothin' around here such as we have rentin' for less than a hunnert dollars a day."

"In the winter?" Lew said.

"Winter, summer, makes no difference."

"Well, if you'll take fifty dollars a day and rent it to me for a week, I'll pay you cash right here and now."

The man held out his hand, palm up.

"You take it, Harvey. I got one more box to load. And make him sign. You make him sign a piece of paper."

"Aw," Harvey said as Lew counted out three one-hundred-dollar bills and then laid a fifty on top.

Harvey counted the money twice, then folded it and slid it into his pocket.

"You clean the place up when you leave now," Harvey said. "And if you stay the winter, we'll settle up come spring. Here's the key. You lock up when you leave and put the key under that big rock yonder." Harvey pointed to a large flat rock under the small front porch.

"Fair enough," Lew said.

He was glad to see the people leave, and he waved at them until they were out of sight. Then he went inside. The cabin had a large front room, nicely furnished, with a rug on the floor that wasn't too worn. There were two large bedrooms, a kitchen, and a storage room. It had a stone fireplace and a cookstove. The cupboards had been cleaned out, except for an old box of baking soda. He found a penny in one of the drawers in the kitchen. And there were two pairs of snowshoes hanging from a peg in the store-room.

"Did you find us a place to stay?" Carol asked when Lew returned to Hardy's less than an hour later. He had stocked the rented cabin with staples, moved some of the cut firewood into the house, put kindling next to the kitchen stove, and made sure there were matches both in the kitchen and in the living room.

"Yes, a nice place."

"Where you got them?" Hardy asked.

"Edge of town. Don't know the people's last names. Harvey and Ruth."

"Them's the Lees. He's a hard-rock miner, still looking for gold, I reckon. What did he soak you?"

"Not much," Lew said, grinning.

"That man Harvey has a heart of pure gold," Jack said. With a wink.

"Thanks for letting Carol stay here," Lew said. "And you're still without a horse."

"No, the man picking me up is bringing me a horse I bought. Like that trotter out there. Missouri-bred, good legs, good bottom. A beauty, really. I've already named him. Want to know what it is?"

"Sure," Lew said.

"Wetzel," Hardy said.

Carol looked puzzled.

"My middle name," Lew said. "The Zanes come from Ohio, Zanesville, Ohio, to be exact. One of my kin, Betty Zane, had a woodsman friend named Lew Wetzel."

"Is that where you got your name?" Carol asked.

"There's more to it than that, but yes. There were rumors that Betty was more than a friend of Wetzel's. Some say she had a child by Lew Wetzel, and the Zane family took him in. Somewhere in that tangle, I was born, and maybe Wetzel was my grandfather. I don't know. I got the name, the Zane family got the scandal."

"That's a terrible name for a horse," Carol said.

"Ain't it, though?" Hardy said. "But it'll remind me of my rescuer, Lew here. And Lew, I want you to know I hold you in the highest respect. Carol here told me that you gave her the money I gave you for renting Leroy. You could have kept the money for yourself. Nobody would have been the wiser. That was a mighty decent thing to do."

"The money belonged to Jeff's kin, not to me," Lew said.

"Still, mighty decent of you. And that job offer I made you still stands. I'd like you to come with me when we ride to Pueblo and Santa Fe."

Lew shook his head. "I've got a heap on my plate right now, Jack. Give the job to somebody else. I don't work easily in harness."

"No, I guess you don't. A man has to follow his own star, I reckon."

"Yes, he does," Lew said, and he missed the glow in Carol's eyes when she looked at him from off to the side. Hardy caught the look, though, and he smiled at her.

"You be careful, Lew," Hardy said. "Miss Carol, I wish you good fortune. You and your kids. They're fine children. I enjoyed meeting them."

"Why, thank you, Mr. Hardy. I'm sure they enjoyed meeting you, too. You certainly kept them entertained."

Lew waved good-bye to Jack and beckoned for Carol to follow him as he rode toward town. Jack waved back and there was a wistful look on his face, as if he might not see any of them again. They met Jack's friend on the way into Leadville. He was leading a tall black trotter wearing a gleaming new Santa Fe saddle, full-rigged, double-cinched, with a rifle scabbard. The saddle was inlaid with silver trim that sparkled in the sun.

"If you spot Don McDermott when we get into town, Carol, I want you to point him out to me. Don't be real obvious about it, but let me know, will you?"

"Why? What are you going to do?"

"I just want to know what he looks like," Lew said.

"I don't believe you."

Lew shrugged. "We'll eat lunch and then I'll take you to your new quarters."

"You can change the subject all you want, Lew Wetzel Zane, but you can't fool me."

"Who's trying to fool you?" he said, and ticked Ruben in the flanks, sending the horse ahead of her and breaking off the conversation.

They ate lunch at the Board of Trade Saloon. Many inside gawked at the woman and her two children. They were seated at a table in a far corner away from the rough-talking men at the bar and sitting at the gambling tables. Lew saw no other women except those that plied patrons for drinks and offered their favors for the afternoon. He ordered steaks and full fare. The children were delighted, and Carol ate as if she had never tasted food before.

Lew scanned the large room as he ate, trying not to show his keen interest. But he wanted them to be seen and talked about.

He wanted the word to spread throughout Leadville that a woman and her two children, a boy and a girl, were there. He wanted to draw Don McDermott out in the open, if he could. If not, he was ready to hunt him down and call him out.

More people gawked at Carol and Lew as they rode through town toward the rented cabin.

"See him?" Lew asked.

"Who?" she said, a teasing look in her eyes.

"You know who."

"Why, I can't imagine."

"You'd tell me if you did, though. Right?"

"If I knew who you were talking about, I might."

"This is serious, Carol."

"Oh, it's serious, is it? Then, no, I haven't seen anyone I know. And I doubt if you have either."

As they passed a dry-goods store, Carol gasped.

She whispered to Lew.

"Don't look now," she said. "But there's Don McDermott, standing in front of that store. And he's looking right at us."

"Which one is McDermott?"

"The big one. He's taller than the others.

He's wearing a red shirt and yellow galluses."

Lew slowed Ruben and scratched the side of his face while he took a look.

He saw the man. More than that, he saw the resemblance to Ed McDermott, the man he had seen in the Double Eagle in Pueblo. They weren't twins, but they were both big men and they resembled each other; the heavy dark brows, the square jaw, the broad shoulders.

"I see him," Lew said out of the corner of his mouth. "Just keep riding and pay him no mind."

"Aren't you going to shoot him?" she teased.

"No, Carol. I'm going to shoot you if you don't settle down and stop taking this as some sort of joke."

"Why, Lew Wetzel Zane, whatever gave you that idea? I'm as serious as you are."

They passed the dry-goods store and headed toward the rented cabin, past other dwellings and wagons rolling out of town.

Lew looked back once they had cleared the commercial district.

No one was following them.

Not yet.

But he knew he would run into Don McDermott again.

And he had a hunch that Carol knew it, too. She fell silent until they reached the cabin.

They dismounted. Lew unlocked the door and the kids rushed inside. Carol lingered for a moment, put a hand on Lew's arm.

"Promise me you'll be careful, Lew, will you?"

"I'm always careful, Carol."

"I wouldn't want anything to happen to you on my account."

"No, ma' am."

"And thanks. Thanks for taking care of us. I just wish . . ."

"What?" he said.

"Nothing."

She rushed past him, into the cabin. Lew stood there a long time, looking back up the road. He felt odd. Carol had stirred something in him that was strange and new. Something he remembered from what seemed long ago, a feeling he'd had for another woman, Seneca.

He felt a burning sensation, a soft warmth on his arm where Carol's hand had touched him. He gulped in air as if to overcome a sudden dizziness, and walked back to the horses, led them around back where the Lees had a small stable that had housed their wagon and mules.

From inside the house, he heard the children laughing and the soft sound of Carol's voice.

Lew felt a tingling in his veins as if he had touched something metal in a winter room after brushing his hand across a blanket.

26

Lew finished cleaning Jeff's Winchester. He stuffed the magazine full of fresh cartridges, worked a shell into the chamber. He handed the rifle to Carol.

"When I'm not here," he said, "you keep this rifle handy at either the front or back door and the shotgun at the other door. Keep the shades down. Don't go outside unless you really have to. If you use the privy, or the kids do, make sure you have a weapon in hand. Keep your eyes open. Keep the doors locked."

"Aren't you going to stay here?" she asked. "There's plenty of room."

"No. I don't think that would be proper. But I'll be close by."

"What does that mean, 'close by'? Are you going to sleep on the rocks out there?"

"I'll be back and forth. I'll take a room in town."

"Lew, you don't have to do that, really. I'd

like you to stay here. I'd feel a whole lot safer, and so would the kids."

"Carol, let it be, please. You'll be all right if you do what I tell you. Be careful. Stay inside as much as you can."

"I'm scared. What you say to me scares me."

Lew looked at her. She didn't look scared, and he doubted that she was. This was a woman with plenty of grit. If she was scared, she hid her fear well.

"You don't have to be scared. I'll be watching over you. From a distance."

"You want Don McDermott to come here after us, don't you?"

"I didn't say that."

"But you do. You're using us as bait."

Lew shook his head. "That's not true. I wouldn't do that. Now, I'm going into town to have a look around, rent me a room, and get settled. Maybe I'll be back for supper. I'll bring you some meat that's already cooked so you don't have to bother with that stove."

"It's a nice place. They have a water pump in the kitchen so I don't have to go out to a well, and you've put in plenty of wood. Bring whatever you want to eat. I'll fix us a nice supper."

"Good," he said. "Now, Leroy is unsaddled, and there was some feed out there. I'll get more. We won't be here more than a few days, maybe."

"You mean we'll be here until you kill Don McDermott, don't you?"

"I didn't say that either."

He said good-bye to Keith and Lynn. Carol acted as if she wanted to kiss him at the front door, but he got out before she had the chance. He wanted her to kiss him, but he was afraid he might not want to leave if she did that. Besides, she was a married woman and he might be taking her all wrong. A man could read too much into a woman's behavior, especially if he was lonely or hadn't been around a good woman for a while.

Lew rode Ruben into town and straight up Harrison Street. He looked for McDermott, but he was no longer in front of Beeker's Dry Goods Emporium. People were still moving out, their wagons and carts full, and he wondered if Leadville would soon be a ghost town. At least, he thought, there should be plenty of hotel rooms to let. He wanted to be in the main part of town where he could see people and they could see him.

He found a livery stable and rented a stall with grain. The place was called Hard Rock Stables, and the man who owned it was a grizzled old-timer named Harry O'Keefe, with rust-white hair, bowed legs, and two days of wiry red stubble on his Irish face.

"You can only have the stall for a week; then I'm boardin' her up, headin' for Pueblo."

"How much?" Lew asked.

"Dollar a day for the stall, fifty cents for the feed. Curryin' and groomin' is extry."

"How much?"

"Two bits."

"Sold," Lew said with a grin.

He walked to the Rocky Mount Hotel and took an upstairs room, paying way too much for a one night's stay. But he put five dollars on the counter and signed the register.

"You can get it cheaper by the week," the clerk said.

"I probably won't be here but a night or two."

"Just sayin'."

"You open all winter?"

"Mister, we never close. We just seal off some of the upstairs rooms that we can't heat and hope some prospectors come down out of the hills and take up board here. There's always a few diehards who stay too long at their claims and get caught by the snow. Once they do get caught, they're mine until the spring thaw."

"I want a second-story room that looks down on Harrison Street," Lew said. "And your name, if you please."

"Leonard Ramsey. And that would be Number 202, just up the stairs, Mr. Zane."

"A question for you, Leonard."

"Feel free."

"Do you know a man named Don Mc-Dermott?"

"Maybe I do, maybe I don't. Why do you ask?"

"He a friend of yours?"

"He a friend of *yours?*" Leonard wasn't going to budge one inch.

"Don's a friend of a friend in Pueblo. Told me to look him up was I in town."

"Who's the friend in Pueblo?"

"You probably don't know him. Wayne Smith."

"Why, no, I don't know him. But he was through here once, seems to me. I know Don, though. Just about everybody round here does."

"Where does he play poker or drink his whiskey? Can you tell me that? I've got time to look him up."

"Just what business are you in, Mr. Zane?"

Lew thought fast. Leonard seemed to be a step ahead of him at every turn.

"I'm a freight hauler," Lew said. "I come

up here to haul ore down to Pueblo."

"Who for?"

"Jack Hardy," Lew said. "Know him?"

"I should say, yes, sir. Well, he must have had a good year is all I can say. Now, what was it you wanted to know about McDermott?"

"Where I can find him."

"Well, he plays cards sometimes at Cy Allen's Monarch Saloon, or at Hyman's. He makes deliveries for the apothecary at Sixth and Harrison and for Beeker, who owns the hardware store. I don't know where he lives, but I heard he stays at the Silver Nugget Hotel over on Fourth Street."

"Thanks, Leonard," Lew said, and took the key to his room, walked upstairs.

He had a good view of Harrison Street. He could see the Opera House from his window, if he leaned out, and some of the saloons where he planned to look for McDermott. When he left the hotel, he walked the streets, getting the lay of the town. He stopped in at both Hyman's and the Monarch, but didn't see the man he was hunting. He went by the apothecary and finally, to the hardware store. He walked out back to the loading dock in the alley.

A man was unloading tools from a wagon. Emblazoned on the side was a legend:

BEEKER EXPRESS. The tools were pickaxes, hoes, shovels, and mauls. They did not look new.

"Those for sale?" Lew asked.

"When they're cleaned up some. Had to take 'em back from some fellers what didn't pay their bill. Go inside and talk to Roy Beeker."

"I will. Say, I thought Don worked here sometimes."

"McDermott? He quit today."

"Quit? How come?"

"I don't know. One minute he was outside, taking him some sun, and then he come in and told Roy he was quitting. You a friend of his?"

"Sort of. I didn't see Don at the apothecary's, either."

"Likely he quit working for Wilbur, too."

"So, where might Don be now, if he's not working?"

"He's got him a gal over on Guadalupe Street. A Mex. They's a cantina there where this gal works. I think her name is Conchita, or something like that."

"What's the name of the cantina?"

"La Huerta. Kind of a dump, you ask me. Full of greasers and hard-luck prospectors. You don't want to go there if you don't really have to."

"Well, thanks."

Lew walked over to Guadalupe Street and started looking for La Huerta. The street was lined with false-front stores with Spanish names. It smelled of baked goods and cheap wine. A lot of the stores were closed, and those that weren't were filled with gaudy trade blankets, Mexican pottery, sausages, wine bottles, and silver jewelry that looked handmade.

At the end of the block, Lew saw the cantina and he could hear music pouring out from inside. Lively guitars, bleating trumpets, drums, and droning basses blasted out a Mexican song. As he approached, some men outside stared at him. They looked to be Mexican and they looked to be drunk. As he started to go inside, one of the men held out his empty palm.

"Dinero, por favor," the Mexican said.

Lew fished a dollar bill out of his pocket and placed it in the man's hand.

"Un mil de gracias."

The man stepped aside and Lew walked into the dark interior of the cantina. Lanterns lit the stage at the back of the large room. People sat at tables, men and women, watching the musicians. Some clapped their hands to the music. Others sang the words of the song. Bleary-eyed men sat at the bar.

One or two looked his way, then turned back to their private conversations.

Lew stepped up to the end of the bar and put his boot up on the rail. There was sawdust on the dirt floor and brass spittoons were placed at empty places along the foot rail. A bartender, a rotund Mexican, noticed him and walked slowly toward him, puffing on a cigarillo.

"Whiskey," Lew said.

The bartender nodded, pulled a bottle from the well, grabbed a shot glass from underneath, set it down, and poured it full.

"Two bits," the bartender said.

Lew nodded and placed coins on the counter. The bartender swiped a quarter from the pile and walked to the cash register, which consisted of two cigar boxes, one for bills, the other for coins.

Once Lew's eyes adjusted to the dim light, he looked around the room. Most of the customers seemed to be Mexicans, but he saw some who were not. These he studied intently. None of them looked familiar.

He raised his glass, put it to his lips.

Someone came through the door behind him. Lew started to turn around when he felt something hard jab into his back.

"I spotted you a block away," a voice said. "You've been dogging me all afternoon."

Lew set down the glass, started to turn around.

The man jabbed him harder.

"You just sit tight until we straighten this all out. What's your play, mister?"

"No play," Lew said. "I'm looking for someone."

"Yeah, I'll bet you are. I seen you before, ain't I?"

"I don't know who you are," Lew said. "Is that a gun in my back?"

"It sure ain't my pecker."

"McDermott?"

"You just said the magic word, mister. Now, who in hell are you and what in hell do you want?"

"If you're McDermott, I've got a proposition for you."

"You were with that Smith woman this mornin'. Her and her kids. She's a married lady."

"I know. How long are you going to stand there behind me?"

"Let's hear your proposition. And it better be good."

The man spoke so low nobody near them could hear him. No one was looking their way. It was odd that McDermott had gotten the jump on him. He must have been in one of the stores or hiding somewhere along

Guadalupe Street, watching Lew all the time. He'd waited, then had come inside the cantina and gotten the drop on Lew. Lew wondered just how far McDermott would go in front of witnesses. He wanted a look at his face, though, before he said another word.

"You'll hear what I have to say after you put away that gun and talk to my face, man to man."

"Tough boy, are you? Why, hell, you ain't hardly dry behind the ears yet. You better talk or I'll let some daylight in that back of yours."

Lew thought fast.

"Carol Smith sent me," he said. "She wants to talk to you. Tonight."

"She does? Me?"

Lew felt the pressure in his back subside as McDermott relaxed.

"Yes. If you want, I'll take you to her."

"Yeah? What does she want to see me about?"

"She wants to give you money, McDermott. She wants you to do her a favor."

"What favor would that be?"

"You'll have to ask her yourself. I'm just the messenger."

McDermott pulled the pistol barrel away from Lew's back.

That was all that he was waiting for. Life or death is decided in an instant sometimes. And sometimes, that instant can seem to last an eternity.

This was one of those times.

Lew struck like a snake and life hung in the balance, teetering on the edge of eternity.

27

Horatio Blackhawk rode into Pueblo before noon, his face glazed with dust, his horse black with sweat. Indian summer gripped the land in one last blaze of heat, and his shirt was soaked with sweat, his hatband dripping salty drops of moisture into his slitted eyes. He picked his way through wagons leaving town, headed for either Denver or Santa Fe, and the main street was clogged with traffic.

The marshal found a nondescript hotel on Hidalgo Street, Hotel Popular, where he got a room and arranged with the clerk for a bath. After he dressed in clean dry clothing, he found a hand laundry and a livery stable. He dropped off his dirty clothes and was promised them the following day. He kept his horse, however, after watering him and brushing him down, and rode to the police station, where he announced himself, showed his credentials, and was ushered into the chief's office.

The chief, wearing a mustard-colored uniform, was short, bald, stocky, with a bulbous nose flanked by red spidery veins that showed the effects of too much drink. He was fanning himself at his desk, pulling on a cigar that belched noxious smoke that smelled like burning rope to Blackhawk.

"I'm Roland Enfante," the chief said. "What can I do for you, Marshal?"

Blackhawk stood there, facing the desk, because Enfante did not indicate either of the two chairs where the marshal might sit.

"I'm looking for two men, Chief. One is not wanted for any crime, name of Jeff or Jeffrey Stevens. The other is a man named Lew Wetzel Zane, wanted for murder of a police officer."

Enfante blinked like some oversized toad. He puffed on his cigar, wreathing his head in a halo of blue smoke. Blackhawk almost expected a small black tongue to dart from between his lips and shiver as it probed for scent.

"Ah. This is recent, yes?"

Blackhawk shrugged. "Probably. Names ring a bell?"

"Um, a bell, yes. I am trying to think of the officer who handled the case. There was a man murdered in a hotel." The chief looked out through the open door and yelled at a policeman sitting at a small table. "Luis, the hotel murder. You know it? Who was the investigator? What hotel? And who was the deceased?"

Luis Acevedo, without looking up from the sheaf of papers in front of him, yelled back.

"Wayne Smith, the Fountain. Deceased, one Jeff Stevens. Suspect, Zane."

"Ah, there you have it, Marshal. A Mr. Jeff Stevens was murdered in his hotel room. He had also been shot, perhaps the day before. He was strangled to death, and his partner, a man named Zane, has disappeared. We are looking for this man."

"Much obliged, Chief," Blackhawk said, and turned to go.

"It is too bad, Marshal Blackhawk, that the man you seek was not captured. Is there a reward?"

"Not that I know of," Blackhawk lied. He did not trust Enfante. And from the look of the other officer, the one at the table, they were overworked and underpaid, which was typical of any police department he had visited.

"Good luck to you, Marshal," Enfante called as Blackhawk strode through the outer office and bent down to open a small gate.

Blackhawk did not reply. His lungs were full of cigar smoke and he yearned for fresh air. But there was none outside. He could smell the odors of the smelters and when he looked up, there were streamers of yellow and brown smoke streaking the airless sky.

Next he went to the Fountain Hotel and spoke to the desk clerk, after identifying himself.

"Do you recall a murder here, within the past week or so, I think, of a man named Jeff Stevens?"

"We'd like to forget that."

"What's your name?"

"John Bascomb."

"Were you on duty when the murder occurred?"

"I was."

"What can you tell me about it?"

"Nothing, really. A man was murdered. The police investigated. The murderer disappeared."

Blackhawk studied the man. He could almost always tell when a man was lying, or covering up something. John Bascomb, he decided, wanted to sweep the murder under the rug and pretend it had never happened.

Or he knew something he didn't want to tell.

"Who determined the cause of death?" Blackhawk said, taking a different tack. Sometimes such a tactic could disarm the witness. Ask an easy question, then get back to the hard ones.

"Ah, we have a surgeon, a physician, who lives in the hotel, Dr. Renfrew. Junius Renfrew. His office is just down the street. He's the one you should talk to, sir."

"I will. Who discovered the body?"

"Well, Dr. Renfrew. The man was his patient, for a gunshot wound."

"He just walked in his room and found him dead?"

"His door was open, yes. Dr. Renfrew said he went to Stevens's room to check on his progress. Mr. Stevens was dead. I was called up to the room as a witness."

"And what did you see?"

Bascomb began to perspire. The furrows on his forehead broke out in beads of sweat, and his sideburns appeared to leak as the perspiration streamed down the edge of his cheek.

"Mr. Stevens was obviously dead. He wasn't breathing or anything. He smelled bad. There was a bandage around his stomach. Then Mr. Zane came in."

"Zane was there?"

"Yes, sir. He said . . . well, I better not say what he said."

"Why is that?"

"Mr. Zane was probably lying. According to the police."

"The police were here, too?"

"One of them came later. Looking for Mr. Zane."

"Oh? Who was this policeman?"

"Uh, Wayne Smith. He said Mr. Zane had shot Mr. Stevens the night before outside the Double Eagle. He said Zane had then choked Mr. Stevens to death while Mr. Stevens was asleep."

"And did Wayne Smith see Mr. Zane?"

"I don't know, sir. Mr. Zane left the hotel and I believe he left town."

"What makes you believe that?"

"Wayne Smith came back and said that Mr. Zane was a fugitive."

"Did Smith say where Zane had gone?"

"No, but my brother Charlie, who works the night shift here, believes that Mr. Stevens was gong to Leadville to see his daughter."

"What made him believe that?"

"I believe he overheard the two men, Mr. Zane and Mr. Stevens, talking about that."

"What happened at the Double Eagle?"

"There was a shooting. Mr. Stevens was shot. Wayne Smith told me that."

"I'd like to see the two rooms these men occupied," Blackhawk said.

"Well, there's nobody in them right now. I suppose you can go up."

Bascomb handed Blackhawk the keys to both rooms. Blackhawk inspected them, didn't find anything of interest.

He went back downstairs and handed the keys back to Bascomb.

"Find anything?" Bascomb asked.

"No. Where can I find Wayne Smith?"

"If he's not at the police station, or investigating, he would be at the Double Eagle. I think he spends his evening hours there."

"I see," Blackhawk said, and walked out of the hotel.

He found Dr. Renfrew's office a few moments later. There was a Mexican woman in the anteroom, and a man with a cane.

"Is the doctor in?" Blackhawk asked the man.

"He's back there. You just sit down and wait like me and her."

Blackhawk ignored him and walked through a door. He heard voices in one of the back rooms. He walked toward them.

Renfrew looked startled when Blackhawk

filled the doorway. He was removing a splinter from a young man's finger. He pulled it out and dropped it into a waste-basket.

"Please wait outside," Renfrew said. "I'll see to you when I can."

"Doctor this boy and send him on his way, Doc. I'm not a patient."

"Police?"

"Something like that."

"Just a minute. Billy, I'm going to clean this and put some salve on it, wrap it up. You keep the dirt out and come back in a week."

"Um-hum," Billy said.

The doctor cleansed the slight wound, packed it with a salve, wrapped a bandage around it, tied it tight, and ushered the young man from the room.

"Now, what's this about, Mr . . ."

"Horatio Blackhawk. I'm a U.S. marshal. I want to talk to you about the death of Jeff Stevens and the man who was with him, Lew Zane."

Renfrew stiffened. He was wearing a white coat, a shirt and tie. He sat on the edge of the examining table, looked at Blackhawk.

"What do you want to know? Mr. Stevens was a patient of mine. For a short time. He died. His body was autopsied. Cause of death, strangulation. The police have the details."

"I heard they believe Zane strangled Jeff Stevens."

"One policeman says that," Renfrew said. "There's no evidence to that effect."

"By one policeman you mean . . ."

"I mean Wayne Smith."

"But you don't believe him?"

"No. Zane wasn't there. I could swear to that. And when he said he had been knocked out, his room keys taken from him, just before Mr. Stevens was murdered, I believed him."

"Why is that, Doctor?"

"I examined a contusion on Mr. Zane's head. It was severe enough for him to lose consciousness. He came up to the room just after Mr. Stevens was killed. I was there, in fact, shortly after the murder. The body was still warm."

"So why do you think Wayne Smith is blaming Zane for the murder?"

"As I understand it, Wayne Smith is, or was, Mr. Stevens' son-in-law."

"Wayne Smith was related to Jeff Stevens?"

"Smith married his daughter. A Carol Smith."

"And where is she?"

"Why, I believe Zane said she was in Leadville."

"Leadville?"

"That's what I understand. Mr. Blackhawk, I have patients waiting."

"Yeah. Thanks. Thanks, Doc. You've been a big help."

Blackhawk left the doctor's office, more puzzled than ever. He went back to the police station, but Smith was not there.

He headed for the Double Eagle. Something wasn't right about the murder of Jeff Stevens. The doctor didn't believe that Zane had murdered him and neither did Blackhawk, after thinking about it. From what Briggs had said, Zane and Stevens were friends. Zane would have no reason to kill Jeff Stevens.

And why was Smith's wife in Leadville when he was in Pueblo? That didn't make sense. It looked to Blackhawk as if Wayne Smith was accusing Zane of everything he could, a shooting at the Double Eagle and a murder at the Fountain Hotel.

This, Blackhawk decided, was the strangest case he had ever investigated.

And Zane? He was either a murderer, or the unluckiest man alive.

28

Lew grabbed the barrel of McDermott's pistol, jerked it from his hand. McDermott made a desperate lunge to retrieve his weapon, but Lew whirled and drove a backhand into McDermott's face, knocking him backward. Then he slashed the butt of the pistol across McDermott's jaw, knocking him to the floor.

Lew flipped the pistol so that he grasped it by the butt. He stooped down, holding the pistol up close to McDermott's face. He cocked the trigger and shoved the barrel up tight against McDermott's upper lip, right under his nose.

The musicians went silent. A hush fell over the room like a heavy blanket.

"Listen to me, you bastard," Lew said, his voice a hoarse rasp laden with rage. "If you ever show your face around Carol Smith and her kids, I'll blow your head off and feed it to the hogs. You got that?"

McDermott said nothing in his dazed state. He stared back at Lew with wet eyes, blood starting to ooze out from the cut in his jaw. The flesh there began to swell and turn red where the pistol had bruised his skin.

"If you think I don't mean business, Mc-Dermott, go dig up your friends at her cabin. They're stone dead and the worms are already eating at them."

Lew stood up, emptied the cartridges out of McDermott's pistol. He worked the lever, pushing each bullet out. In the silence of the cantina, each bullet made a distinct clanking sound as it fell into an empty spittoon. Lew dropped the empty pistol into the same spittoon.

At that moment, a young Mexican woman rushed up and knelt by McDermott. She cradled his head in her hands and spat out a stream of Spanish invective at Lew. McDermott stretched his hand out toward the spittoon, sliding his arm under the woman's skirt as if to conceal it.

"Conchita, *ten cuidado*," another woman said as she approached.

Conchita stopped cursing as McDermott's hand fluttered above the spittoon, stabbing for the butt of his pistol.

Lew stepped in and brought his boot heel

down hard on McDermott's arm. McDermott cried out in pain. His arm shrank back under Conchita's skirt, and she rose to strike Lew with her tiny fist balled up like a darning egg.

Lew sidestepped her and headed toward the door, his right hand hovering near the butt of his pistol.

He glanced at the patrons in the cantina, looking for anyone who appeared to be ready to fight. No one challenged him, and he walked to the door in three long strides. Conchita assailed him with a fresh string of Spanish curse words, shaking her fist at him and spitting into the air.

Lew breathed easier once he was outside. The Mexican beggars melted away from him as he strode down the street. The cantina burst into a hubbub of voices all shouting at once.

But nobody emerged from La Huerta, and nobody followed him.

When he showed up at the cabin where Carol and her children were staying, it was late in the afternoon and the sky was scudding over with white thunderheads. They seemed to rise from the bowels of the mountains, bright in the sun, brighter than the white show that shone on the highest peaks.

He was on horseback and he carried a haunch of cooked pork, a hank of sugar beets, a sack of squash, and sweet candies for the children, licorice sticks and chocolate caramel balls the size of quail eggs.

The clouds turned dark and shadowed the valley by the time Lew and Carol sat down to supper with the kids.

"It's going to snow tonight," Carol said.

"You think so?"

"Yes, yes, yes, snow," sang Lynn.

"A snowman," Keith said. "A big snowman."

"The food is delicious," Carol said. "Thanks, Lew. I wish you didn't have to stay in town tonight. You might have to dig us out tomorrow."

Lew smiled, but said nothing.

When they were finished, they heard a rumbling sound.

"That's not thunder," Lew said.

"It sounds like thunder," Carol said.

They all went outside and stood there, watching the long line of wagons heading out of Leadville. A mist hung over the town and the wagons emerged out of that heavy gauze, made even darker by the black thunderheads.

"Taking the ore down to the smelters at Pueblo," Lew said. The kids waved to the drovers and ran around like excited birds, jumping up and down.

"They've never seen anything like it," Carol said. "It's like a parade to them. And they've never seen a parade, either."

On and on, the wagons rolled by as the sky grew darker, and then the first flakes of snow started to fall.

And still the wagons came, as the snowfall grew thicker.

Finally, in the rear of the caravan, Lew saw a man on a black trotter. The man waved.

"Who's that?" Carol asked.

"Hard to see, but I think it's Jack Hardy."

"Oh, yes, I recognize him now. He's coming this way."

Hardy left the wagon train and rode over to the cabin.

"Lew," Hardy said as he reined up.

"Jack."

"You better git while the gittin's good. Goin' to be a helluva snow tonight."

"We'll leave in the morning."

"We're hoping to outrun it. I took up the rear so I might have easier going. Wagons will keep the road clear for a good long time."

"See you in Pueblo, maybe," Lew said.

"Watch yourself, Lew. I saw Don McDermott at Beeker's dry goods and hardware store when I was leaving. I went in to buy a couple of shovels. He was buying something, too."

"What was he buying?"

"Dynamite."

"Dynamite?"

"That's what I said. And he's an experienced powder man. You watch your back."

"I will."

"McDermott's not going to blow him a mine shaft, Lew."

"I'll keep that in mind."

Hardy waved good-bye and turned his horse, rode back to the wagons, caught up with his lead drover. He disappeared in the mist and snow, which was falling faster and thicker than before.

"What did all that mean?" Carol asked. "What Mr. Hardy was telling you about McDermott."

"Oh, probably nothing. I ran into McDermott today and told him to leave you alone. I think he got the message."

"You did? Was there trouble?"

"No. Just conversation."

He said good-bye to Carol a few minutes after the last wagon rolled out of sight and they were left in the silence of the snowfall. He told her to be ready to ride out in the morning.

"I wish you wouldn't go, Lew."

"It's only for a night. See you early in the morning."

He wanted to stay. Carol wanted him to stay. But he wanted to give McDermott enough rope to hang himself, and he could only do that by leaving and hoping McDermott would be watching him ride back into Leadville.

The road was still fairly clear, but the snow was accumulating along the sides. When he rode into town, all the roofs were white. They gleamed like linen sheets in the darkness. Only a few places were still open, and their lamps glowed through the falling snow like orange beacons.

He rode to the livery stable, but did not go in. He dismounted and waited a few minutes. He heard a horse galloping down Harrison Street, heading east out of town. Then the quiet returned. Lew climbed back up on Ruben after he put on his winter coat. He pulled the rifle from its scabbard and saw that it was still dry.

He rode to high ground and headed east, riding above the town, heading back toward the cabin where Carol and the children were.

Ruben picked his way through the trees,

dislodging a few rocks as he clung to the sloping hillside. Lew's heart started pounding as they neared the cabin. Finally, there it stood, isolated, detached from any other signs of civilization, its windows glowing a pale orange through the heavy mist and the falling flakes of snow.

He tied Ruben to a scrub pine, drew the rifle from its sheath, and walked down behind the cabin. He was close enough that he could hear the voices of the children. They were at one of the windows, looking out at the snow. Every so often, he could hear Carol comment on something they said.

But Lew's ears were attuned to a different type of sound. He didn't expect McDermott to ride up to the house, but he had a strong feeling that he would show up, probably on foot.

He heard a horse whicker on the other side of the road.

"Please don't put out those lamps," Lew whispered to himself. If the house went dark, he knew he wouldn't be able to see a thing.

Finally, he heard the crunch of boots on stone. He strained his ears to pinpoint which direction they were coming from as they grew louder and louder.

He saw a shadow moving through the curtain of snow. A man was walking toward the cabin.

Lew cocked the rifle, holding the trigger in slightly so that it didn't make enough noise for the approaching man to hear it.

Then, when the man was within thirty yards of the front of the cabin, he stopped.

Lew licked his dry lips.

A bright flame flared as the man struck a match. For a brief moment, the fire illuminated the man's face. Don McDermott. He touched the match to something, and Lew saw sparks spew out into the darkness.

A fuse.

McDermott let it burn for two or three seconds until the fire was racing down the fuse. Then he drew his arm back and threw it overhand toward the cabin. The fuse made a fiery arc, streaming golden sparks behind it as it sped toward the cabin.

Lew brought his rifle to his shoulder and took dead aim on McDermott.

He squeezed the trigger and the rifle jumped in his hand, bucked against his shoulder.

Lew dropped his rifle and ran toward the cabin. He didn't even look toward McDermott. He'd heard the bullet hit something and then heard a sound like a body falling.

There were a half-dozen sticks of dynamite tied together.

The fuse was burning short when Lew came upon it. He knew he had only a second or two to either put out the fire by pinching the fuse, or toss the lethal bundle as far as he could throw it.

The fuse sizzled like a hissing snake as Lew bent over to pick up the sticks of dynamite.

Each second seemed to last a thousand hours as the fuse burned down to the blasting cap.

A lifetime passed in the agony of that last second of life.

The hissing stopped and there was dead silence in that same passage of hours and years and lifetimes.

An eternity in a single tick of a man's pocket watch.

29

Just as Lew's hand grabbed the dynamite, the front door opened behind him. Then a shot exploded from where McDermott had been a few moments before. A bullet plowed a furrow in front of Lew as he threw the sticks of dynamite toward the road. A shotgun blasted from behind him, spewing orange sparks into the night.

The dynamite exploded in midair, a huge blast that knocked Lew to the ground, burst in his eardrums with deafening force. For a single vivid moment, he saw McDermott staggering toward him, pistol in hand. He lit up like a wax figure in a lighted gallery, and then disappeared as the fire in the sky went out, smothered by snow, its many brilliant sparks extinguished as they fell to earth.

Lew looked over his shoulder, saw Carol standing in the lighted doorway of the cabin, a smoking shotgun in her hands.

"Get back inside," Lew yelled, then turned back to McDermott.

He heard the front door slam shut, cutting off the shaft of light that had partially illuminated McDermott. Lew saw a shadow through the white drapes of the snow. The man was still coming toward him, his right arm outstretched. Lew jumped to his feet and drew his Colt, surprising even himself with his speed.

McDermott fired his pistol.

Lew saw him clearly in the bright orange flash from the pistol's muzzle, saw him for an instant as his weapon spat death at him. Lew went into a crouch and held his pistol with both hands to steady his aim, something he had practiced for months back home.

Lew squeezed the trigger even as there was the chilling sound of a bullet whizzing past his ear, a ghostly rustle of wind in the eerie whiteness of the dark. McDermott vanished as the muzzle flash disappeared. In place of his shadow, Lew saw only the orange afterglow of the pistol blast, a maddening vision that burned through his pupils and etched itself like a splash of acid in his brain.

"Arrrgh," McDermott grunted.

Lew sidestepped from his position, then

charged ahead several paces.

And there, looming out of the snowy ink of night, McDermott reappeared, still standing, his pistol at the ready, staring at the lighted cabin.

McDermott was hit. Lew could see that by the way the man swayed to keep his balance. How badly, Lew did not know.

McDermott spotted Lew at that moment and swung his pistol.

Too late.

Lew stopped, crouched, and fired. The range was no more than a dozen feet.

The hammer of the Colt struck the primer, exploding the powder in the cartridge. Flame and lead burst from the muzzle at over nine hundred feet per second, striking McDermott with the energy of a wrecking ball. McDermott staggered backward with the impact of the bullet. His gun hand went limp with the shock of it and his pistol dropped onto the snowy ground.

McDermott crumpled, a blank look on his face, a vacancy creeping into his eyes like a soft mist. Lew stood over him, holding his Colt close to McDermott's left cheek. He thumbed back the hammer, breathing hard and fast, his temples throbbing with the rush of blood.

"Damn you, McDermott, I warned you to leave Carol alone."

"Who . . . who in hell are you?" McDermott babbled, staring at Lew with cloudy eyes as the pain stabbed at his senses.

A wind, seemingly risen from nowhere, blew past the two men. The snow swirled around them, the flakes like dervishes dancing a macabre series of pirouettes around the two men. McDermott slumped onto the back of his legs until he was in a kneeling position.

Lew's finger caressed the trigger. It would only take a slight squeeze to blow McDermott's brains to mush.

"Death wind," McDermott murmured. "A wind of death . . ."

Lew heard footsteps behind him. He looked up and there was Carol, the shotgun in her hands. She was staring at McDermott like a woman in a trance.

She looked like a wraith in her pale nightgown, the wind making it flap and then plastering it to her form until Lew could almost see through it.

"Death . . ." McDermott said, and pitched forward, smashing his face into the patina of snow that lay on the ground.

Lew eased the hammer back down and slid his Colt back in its holster. He knelt down and put two fingers just under Mc-Dermott's ear, feeling for the pulse.

There was none.

"Is he . . ." Carol stammered.

"He's dead," Lew said.

The shotgun in her hands dipped as she relaxed, the barrels pointing to the ground at a forty-degree angle. Lew stood up and she ran to him, pressed against him. He could feel her body tremble against his. Then she began to shiver with the cold.

The brief wind stopped and the snow fell straight down, faster and faster, thicker and thicker, until they stood in a white vortex of nothingness, a lump of a man at their feet, his back turning white as the snow clung to his coat.

"What did he mean?" she said.

"I don't know."

"That sudden wind. Was it . . ."

"I don't know," he said again. "Let's go inside before you freeze to death."

"Yes, yes. Inside."

She seemed dazed as Lew walked her back to the cabin. The door was open and the children stood there in bewilderment, like two orphan waifs come to beg in their long nightgowns.

Lew pushed Carol inside.

"I'll be back," he said. "I've got to get my

horse in out of the weather. Lock the door."

"Hurry," she said.

Lew walked away, the snowflakes touching his face like cool kisses from silken lips. He retrieved his rifle, then walked a zigzag course up the slope. Ruben whinnied as he came near. Lew patted his neck and untied the reins. He and the horse walked back down the slope, which was turning slippery under their feet.

Lew carried only his rifle when he knocked on the cabin door.

Carol opened it and he stepped inside, snow swirling in his path. She closed the door.

"I left my bedroll in town," he said.

"You won't need it, Lew. Set your rifle down and let me take your hat. The children are in bed and I've brewed some fresh coffee."

"I should —"

"Shhhsh," she whispered and took his hat, set it on a chair. She took his hand and led him to the divan.

It was snug inside the cabin. Carol had a fire blazing in the hearth. He could see the snowflakes dancing against the windowpanes, melting as they struck, leaving tiny streaks of water, like snail tracks, on the glass.

And there was no wind outside. Only the gently falling snow.

It was quiet in the Double Eagle that afternoon when U.S. Marshal Horatio Blackhawk sat down with Wayne Smith for his first interview with the policeman.

While they were talking, Blackhawk remembered a report he had seen when he was working in Springfield. It was a police report from Bolivar, Missouri, regarding theft by a man named Wayne Smith. And Smith, according to the report, was a fugitive from the law.

But Blackhawk said nothing to Smith. He regarded him with the cold dispassionate eye of a lawman as he had been trained to do.

Smith was a pasty-faced man with long sideburns, attesting to his vanity, a neatly trimmed, pencil-thin moustache, and a squirrel's tail of a small beard flourishing at the point of his pointed chin. He had small, deep-set eyes so pale and blue they looked dead. Smith was thin and wiry, cocky as an Irish sailor home on leave.

"So, you think this Lew Zane murdered your father-in-law, Jeff Stevens?" Blackhawk said after a few moments of silence in their conversation.

"Dead sure of it. I'd like to see the bastard hang. Jeff was a good old fella."

"What makes you so sure Zane did it?"

"Hell, he was the one rode with Jeff. He had the opportunity. Probably robbed him."

"Do you have any idea where Zane might be now?"

Smith took a sip of whiskey. He was off duty. Blackhawk was nursing a whiskey of his own.

"I heard tell he went up to Leadville. I'll get him. One of these days."

"And you'll arrest him?" Blackhawk asked.

"Damned right. And I'll see him hang."

"What about your wife, Smitty? Isn't she up in Leadville?"

A nervous twitch worked the muscle under one of Smith's eyes.

"She'll be coming down any day now. They had a snow up in the mountains, but the roads ought to be clear."

"You think Zane will show up here in Pueblo?"

"Sooner or later."

Blackhawk left it at that. He knew who Wayne Smith was and he could keep for the time being. In fact, Smith might be the man to draw Zane out in the open if he did come back to Pueblo.

When Blackhawk left the Double Eagle,

he rode straight to the Grand Hotel, where he had an appointment with a man from Leadville, John Jacob Hardy, otherwise known as "Jack."

"That was quite a display you put on today, Mr. Hardy," Blackhawk said as they talked over whiskeys in the hotel bar. It was dark, with a pale sun slanting through the stained-glass windows of the saloon. "Those silver bars looked mighty tempting to a few people."

"Call me Jack, Marshal. And they sure as hell don't call you Horatio, do they?"

"None do."

"Well, that display was for the short-lived pleasure of a member of Pueblo's finest, one Wayne Smith. I think Smith plans to pull off a robbery of that silver down around Spanish Peaks when we haul it to Santa Fe. Only, I've got a surprise for Mr. Smith. When he attacks us, he'll get no silver. Only hot lead."

"Do you know Smith's wife? She was in Leadville, I understand."

"Met her. Got two kids."

And that's when Hardy told Blackhawk about the insurance policy Smith had taken out on Carol. He told him about Don McDermott and a man named Lew Wetzel Zane.

"So you think this Zane feller is with Wayne's wife?"

"He was looking after her and the kids."

"I want you to do me a favor, Jack," Blackhawk said.

"Glad to. What is it?"

"Hold off on going to Santa Fe until after Zane and the Smiths come down from Leadville."

"How come?"

"I'll let you know later. You might not have to worry about Wayne Smith robbing you."

"Are you going to arrest him?"

Blackhawk smiled.

"Who knows what will happen," he said.

The day came when Lew brought Carol and her children down to Pueblo. The snow on the foothills had melted and they stood stark and mottled in the sunlight. The high peaks were still mantled in snow, but the roads were passable.

Lew's stomach quivered with the sensation of flying insects. Carol had told him that she was going to divorce Wayne the minute she got to Pueblo. Lew had made no comment. He had fallen in love with her, but he knew Wayne wasn't going to give her up. Not without a fight. And he might even try and kill her.

She was tense, too, he knew. They had been through a lot, but now they both faced the unknown.

They rode up to the Fountain Hotel.

Carol didn't notice a man standing in the shadows, across the street. But Lew saw him. He saw the shiny badge on the man's vest, the way he slouched against the building with his tall, lanky frame, his right hand free, lazing next to his low-slung holster.

Blackhawk looked at Zane, then touched a finger to the brim of his hat.

Zane returned the salute.

Blackhawk smiled.

And waited.

The employees of Thorndike Press hope you have enjoyed this Large Print book. All our Thorndike and Wheeler Large Print titles are designed for easy reading, and all our books are made to last. Other Thorndike Press Large Print books are available at your library, through selected bookstores, or directly from us.

For information about titles, please call:
  (800) 223-1244

or visit our Web site at:
  http://gale.cengage.com/thorndike

To share your comments, please write:
  Publisher
  Thorndike Press
  295 Kennedy Memorial Drive
  Waterville, ME 04901